"You don't care about anything!" he accused

Hugo's fingers dug into her shoulders as he turned her around to face him. She gazed at him, and he returned her gaze coolly, fixedly, until she was forced to lower her lashes. Then his mouth was on hers.

Tirza was powerless to stop herself from responding, and she satisfied the longing to touch the firm skin beneath his shirt, opening it so that she could feel his body against her own. She freed her lips from his and buried her face in his chest.

His fingers turned her face upward so that he could go on kissing her. She was only vaguely aware of the faraway cry of some animal. Her world had narrowed to nothing more than the hard close circle of Hugo's arms.

Peacock in the Jungle

by

WYNNE MAY

Harlequin Books

TORONTO • NEW YORK • LOS ANGELES • LONDON
AMSTERDAM • PARIS • SYDNEY • HAMBURG
STOCKHOLM • ATHENS • TOKYO • MILAN

Original hardcover edition published in 1982
by Mills & Boon Limited

ISBN 0-373-02532-7

Harlequin Romance first edition February 1983

CHAPTER ONE

TIRZA's father was a rich man. His money came from office and departmental store complexes, high-rise housing complexes and a sheep farm in the semi-desert.

Her mother had been Cecilia Theron, before her marriage, and she had died in India.

Her childhood had been spent in luxury, if in loneliness. After her mother's death she and her father had returned to South Africa and had divided their time between the Dutch-style mansion in Cape Town, a chalet in the Drakensberg mountains and a house, all steel, glass and open galleries, hugging the dunes to one side of the headland of the Robberg, which juts out into the Indian Ocean.

She did much on impulse and, at twenty-three, followed the dictates of fashion, more for her own amusement than from any sense of obligation. She also adored wearing sheer silk shirts and lacy tanga briefs beneath immaculate denims. When she shopped she never bought anything she did not like. There was a tiny gap between her two front teeth and her face, fabulous tawny hair, green eyes, slim body and unusual husky voice had all been described, and dissected, by countless magazines. People stared after her because she was Douglas Harper's daughter.

At the moment she was sitting on a high stool in a ladies' cocktail bar in a Holiday Inn on the

Eastern Boulevard in Cape Town. The bar was smelling of smoke, liquor and perfume, but it was select and the women in it elegant and escorted. A young man with a moody and sarcastic kind of face was playing an organ and when he started to sing Tirza's slim, tanned fingers tightened round the glass she was holding and turning round and round on the counter. As she tilted her head forward, her tawny hair slid over her cheeks, as she had intended it to do, and her dark lashes screened the hurt in her green eyes.

On the stool, next to her, Nigel Wright went on talking . . . and talking, and she tried to switch her mind off him, off what he was saying. She didn't want to listen to him, but the words kept hammering at her brain.

'I intended telling you,' he was almost whining, she found herself thinking bitterly, 'I was playing for time.' Vaguely, she was aware of his shoulders lifting. 'I mean, it's only been a month . . . we've only known one another for a month.'

'A month in which you gave me no indication that you were married.' Her voice was ice-cold.

Nigel took a breath and expelled it immediately. 'Look, Tirza, I know it might have been a bit premature to ask you to go away with me, but the offer was too tempting to say no. I mean, I could never afford to lash out on a place like this for two whole weeks. It seemed to come up at the right moment. Think . . . two weeks, with nothing to do but to get to know one another . . . what's so wrong in that?'

'With nothing to do except make love, because,

of course, you were asking me to live with you for two weeks, during which time you might or might not have deemed it necessary to tell me that you are married. But in any case, I would have refused your offer, wife or no wife. It's a pity I found out, though, isn't it? You could have gone on playing for time. I kept this date with you this evening merely to let you know that I've found out. I never want to see you again—okay? I don't know what gave you the opinion that I'm easy game.'

'Perhaps because you're a model,' he said, his voice nasty.

'Oh, I see . . . because I'm a model. Thank you very much!' She turned to look at him. 'I can't get over you,' she said. 'How naïve can you *get*?'

She modelled for Harper's, when she felt like it, and for the small boutique in which she had an interest.

At the organ, the young man was singing his heart out. Automatically, Tirza found herself listening to the words. If you've been hurt, make up your mind, I'm sure you'll find, someone who would ree . . . ly lu . . . huh . . . ve you.

Suddenly she had a vision of a small girl without a mother, and then a teenager who desperately needed a woman's hand and to turn to for advice. And then, later again, a girl who had been hurt once, at twenty, and now again at twenty-three. Being Tirza Harper was not all a bed of roses.

'Tirza,' Nigel felt for her hand.

'Leave me alone!' She snatched her hand away and the fingers of her other hand searched her cheekbones to reassure herself that there were no tears there. 'Will you leave me *alone*?' Her voice was low and tense. 'I don't want you here.'

After a moment he said, 'How will you get home?'

'Being a *model*, I'm quite capable of seeing myself home.'

She was aware that the man on the stool next to her own had stopped talking to a male companion and had turned his head to look at her. In the dimly-lit room their eyes met, before she turned away, flustered.

'For the last time, are you coming?' Nigel was getting to his feet.

'No. You go back to your wife.'

'Okay, if that's the way you want it, but it doesn't necessarily have to be my wife, believe me.'

'I can quite believe that. Personally, however, I'm beginning to find this extremely boring. Would you mind leaving?' She gave him her back.

Vaguely, she was aware of Nigel leaving the bar and she felt suddenly lost—a stranger among strange faces. To calm herself she concentrated on the man on the stool next to her own. Long legs, encased in elegant trousers. The hand on the counter, moving a glass this way and that, was well formed and tanned. She stole a glance at his profile. Hmmmm . . . women would find him an irresistible force. His hair was well styled and longish in the neck.

'We were lucky to get hold of her,' he was saying. 'She can match up and dye any and just about every conceivable shade and colour, ranging from pastel to exotic vibrance. Actually, I'll be leaving again for Swaziland the day after tomorrow.'

Listening to him, Tirza thought that there was an indefinable magnetism about him, even in this dim light. It was obvious that he was the symbol of cool, self-reliant masculinity. Was he the kind of man who would cause a thrill of fear by asking a girl to go away with him for two weeks at a 'fantastic place', overlooking the sea? And was he married, too, into the bargain?

Suddenly he turned and their eyes met. That he had been aware of her scrutiny was obvious, and it showed in the way his eyes held hers for a long disturbing moment before they left her face and went over her briefly. She could tell by their expression that he thought she was trying to pick him up. Even in this light she saw that his skin had a matt Mediterranean kind of tan.

He fixed a steely gaze upon her. 'Do I know you?' he asked, in just the kind of voice she had imagined him to have.

'No. I'm sorry.' She was embarrassed. 'I'm ashamed to admit it, but I was eavesdropping. You see, I gathered that you must have been discussing the weaving industry.'

His eyes, she saw, were dark blue and there was an almost hostile glint in them, so she said, 'It doesn't matter.'

'Oh, but I can assure you it does matter. You see, I *was* discussing the weaving industry, and into the bargain I was also eavesdropping.'

'Oh?' Tirza gave him a troubled glance.

'Cheer up,' he went on. 'Maybe he'll come back.'

'I see. Well, he won't.' Her voice was unfriendly.

'You'll rustle up someone else, I guess. *Models* always do, somehow.' A flicker of something like amusement crossed his face.

'That's not very funny!' she answered angrily.

'I'm sure you're an expert.' This time he smiled. 'Models always are, aren't they?'

'You've got a nerve!' she snapped.

He shrugged. 'I happened to hear one or two things, during the course of the evening.' His eyes went to her empty glass. 'Let me buy you a drink.'

Feeling humiliated and a little sick, she reached for her bag, which was on the counter beside her glass. 'That's not why I spoke to you,' she said.

His companion had left the bar, she noticed, and the dimly lit space was awash with conversation and soft laughter. Her green eyes were angry and to him she turned again. 'You spoke to me like that because you heard me say that I model. Right?'

'Well, yes.' He shrugged casually. 'I guess if I'm honest I'll admit it. I'm right, aren't I?' When he laughed harshly, Tirza realised that he was goading her and, ruffled, she turned away. She stared down at her glass, which was empty—the way she felt—and started to move it about, waiting until she felt composed enough to get up and leave. Suddenly the glass shot out from between her tense fingers and landed on the carpet between the two stools.

'Allow me,' he said and, seething, she watched him retrieve it. Looking at her, he said directly, 'I know *I* need another drink and seeing that you've been sounding like a sighing epidemic here, beside me, I guess you need one too. Right?'

'I don't need a drink,' she said. 'I'm about to leave, as a matter of fact.'

'Look,' he said, 'I have no objection to models. Besides,' his blue eyes travelled almost insolently over her, 'you *weave*.' He laughed softly.

'And that makes it all right, I suppose? The good old-fashioned art of weaving. In any case, I don't weave. I'm merely interested in the weaving industry.'

'About having a drink with me—be charitable and forget what you *think* I meant,' he said. 'I heard you tell him to get lost, or words to that effect. You're upset, I realise that now.'

Tirza watched him as he signalled the barman and then he turned to her again. 'What were you drinking?'

She asked for a fruit juice. 'But I'll pay for it,' she told him.

After he had given their order he said, 'When I become aware of a chic, tawny-haired girl, with an elusive accent and a personal sense of style, having a set-to right next to me with a married man I quite obviously find myself becoming curious. And then, when that man walks off and leaves her— even when she's told him to do just that—I'm more than just a little curious.'

'In a generation where talking to a strange man in a dimly-lit bar doesn't seem to matter, I nevertheless never trade on the fact,' Tirza told him. 'This situation, therefore, is outside my experience. It's just that,' she broke off and lifted her shoulders, 'I've had a terrible day. At the moment I feel . . .' she shook her head and smiled, '*old*, and lost, into the bargain. I suppose it does help to talk, right now.'

Their drinks arrived and she insisted on paying for her own, and he watched her with some amusement. After a moment he said, 'Well, here's to the weaving industry.'

Smiling, she raised her glance in response. 'But I don't weave. I know about looms and—things— but I don't weave. Right?'

'What things?' He sounded genuinely interested.

'Well, for one thing, the superfine mohair that goes into looms.'

'So, in other words, you've modelled garments which have been made from superfine mohair.'

'Yes.' She glanced down at her glass. She was thinking that she could have told him about her father who bought straight from the weavers for his many departmental stores—garments, curtaining, tapestries, carpets—but she remained silent. Apart from the fact that the man beside her was a stranger, she hardly ever spoke about her father. If she had been so inclined, she could have told him that her father just also happened to own a farm in the Karroo, where mohair was produced and marketed to Port Elizabeth, processed in Uitenhage and reached the factories in 'top' form, which meant that the hair was taken from the top of the angora goat, where it was longest. The mohair arrived in a condensed top form to be spliced and spun. Before she had become interested in that side of her father's business, she had been bored nearly to tears over many a dinner table while her father went on and on about such things, always getting to his sore point, which was her brother Howard, who was living in Portugal, when he should have been living at home and taking an interest in the many Harper concerns.

Their hands were so close on the bar counter that they were almost touching and Tirza was aware of the warmth of his, spreading towards her own.

She decided to go on. 'I have a knowledge of looms and weavers and spinners and dyers—now you can see why I began eavesdropping—and I also have a knowledge of modelling, which, by the way, does not place me in the role of a fool.'

'Let me put it this way. Only a fool would go on talking to a stranger in a smoky ladies' cocktail bar on the Eastern Boulevard . . . don't you think?' His eyes were remarkable, she thought, of so deep a blue as to appear black at first sight.

There was a troubled set to her shoulders when she answered him. 'That's not very funny.' Her voice was suddenly drained. 'Personally, I'm beginning to find this very tiresome.'

'I'm just being realistic. How are you getting home, by the way? Now that it seems very clear that he's not coming back.'

'What would you like to hear me say? That I'm going to hitch?' She was wearing an elegant ribbed top, with silk trousers, and the result was one of provocative sophistication. An elaborate gold bracelet at her wrist, a gift from her father, hinted at money. The heritage bequeathed to her by her beautiful mother was always evident in the way she wore her clothes. 'Anyway,' she went on, 'your opinion of me is not important.'

They were silent, each assessing the other. For the moment Nigel Wright was completely forgotten.

'I'm about to leave,' those dark blue eyes continued to hold her gaze, 'and it just happens that I'm a-passing thataway.'

'Are you now?' Her voice was very unfriendly. 'And whataway would that be? It's probably right out of your way.'

'Then that's a chance I'll have to take, isn't it? Along with the chance you'll have to take, if you decide to come.'

A stubborn streak in her caused her to reply, 'What chance would I be taking?' Because she had no power of them, her green eyes went to his mouth and she was aware of a current of communication between them, razor-sharp and shocking, almost, in its vibrant message.

'For one thing, the risk involved in accepting a lift from a complete stranger, even though we've broken the ice, as they say.'

'Risks and danger are two things I take very lightly,' she felt compelled to goad him. 'Nevertheless, I have absolutely no intention of accepting a lift from you. I'm quite capable of fending for myself. I happen to be very independent, and it's not just something to do with male chauvinism or Women's Lib. I do hand it to you that men can do certain things better than women and I have no desire to dominate—but, and I want to make this quite clear, I can get around to handling my own transport home.' Her tawny hair swirled round his face. 'You're not talking to a person of limited intelligence. Excuse me.' She stood up and when she glanced at him she was quick to notice that she had ruffled him at last, and she enjoyed the little moment of triumph.

She was standing waiting for attention from the desk, when he came through to the foyer, and there was a haughty look about her and she looked dramatic and beautiful. Coming up to her, he said, 'There are no risks involved.' There was a degree of annoyance in his voice. 'You can tell me where to go.'

Beside him, she was slim and excitingly long, although not very tall. Her narrowness was provoking, somehow, and one or two men glanced at her with interest. Men seemed to find her slim body disturbing and she had seen it in their faces from the time she was very young. The knowledge chilled rather than thrilled her.

There was a moment of stiff silence before she said, 'All right. Thank you.' She knew that, if she had to be honest with herself, she would prefer to go with him than to get into a taxi by herself.

His car was parked in the parking area and as they walked towards it, the wind caught at her hair and sent it flying across her face, so she turned, for a moment, into the wind, holding her face up so that her hair was swept back. Catching hold of it with one hand, she began walking again. Taking her arm, he guided her in the direction of his Alfa-Romeo and she waited for him to unlock the door

for her, conscious of him all the while. With his
dark tan, blue eyes and good looks, he would, she
found herself thinking, invariably overcome the
resistance of women of all ages. Against her will
she had even been conscious of his aggressively
masculine walk beside her. Also, he had the kind
of face which would, whenever he felt so inclined,
give nothing away. He brushed against her as he
stood to one side for her to slide into the seat, and
she found herself wondering whether this had been
accidental.

The lights of the foreshore were winking and
throbbing and glittering on the black water.
Everything was vibrant and jewel-like with colour.
In the far distance, a jet airliner had taken to the
black space over the airport and she could see its
light jump, jump, jumping. Her thoughts went to
Nigel. Would he turn out to be just a mirage?
Looking back briefly, she realised that he had
always been very cagey and on edge when talking
about himself. What a little fool she had been! All
the time he had been dining, wining, dancing and
swimming with her he had been cheating her.

The confined space of the car was invaded by
the fragrance of her perfume and when her companion got in beside her he said, 'Your perfume—I
like it. By the way, my name is Hugo Harrington.'
When she remained silent he turned to look at her.

'Tirza,' she told him.

After a moment he said, 'Where to, Tirza?'

'Bishopscourt, please.' She moved the heavy gold
bracelet up and down her wrist.

When they were on their way she said, 'You

know, being a model, if only part-time, would appear to ban one from being a legitimate member of society, at times.'

'Did I imply that?' He turned to look at her.

'No, but the tone of your voice suggested it.'

'As it so happens my business relies heavily on the rag trade—and the modelling that goes along with it.' He turned to look at her. 'That surprises you, doesn't it? As a matter of fact, it was for this reason I wondered whether we'd met before when I heard you talking to your boy-friend about being a model. I wasn't eavesdropping for nothing.' The tone of his voice was mocking.

'As a matter of fact,' asked Tirza, her curiosity getting the better of her, 'what exactly *did* you hear?'

'Do you really want to know?'

'I wouldn't be asking if I didn't.'

'I was able to come to the conclusion that you resented the fact that many of those little intimacies you'd been sharing with him have been shared with his wife.' His voice was casual, but she knew that he was waiting for her reply.

'I see.'

'I was also interested to hear that you model.'

'I was aware of your scrutiny, of course.' Her voice was cool. 'You thought, because I was looking at *you*, I was trying to pick you up.'

'Strong words, but I was amused by the possibility. I was going to offer you a job, actually.' His voice was casual, but she was aware of being appraised by those blue eyes.

'That was very generous of you.' She did not try to hide the sarcasm.

'I'll be honest with you,' he went on, 'it didn't take me long to realise that what you were going through, sitting there beside me, was nothing short of an inner upheaval.'

'I knew, when I went there tonight with him, that I was going to have to arrange my own transport home, as it so happened,' she told him. 'I went there to quarrel with him.'

'And it just so happened that you preferred me to some taxi-driver. Right?'

'Yes.' Having made her point she was silent.

After a while he said, 'Keep me informed as to the route.'

'I was just going to tell you to turn left at the top of the hill. You'll see the huge wrought-iron gates.'

The iron gates to her father's white Cape-style mansion were closed and, before getting out to open them, Hugo Harrington let out a low whistle. 'Papa has money,' he said.

'If he has, it's something *I* never talk about,' she replied very coolly, thinking of the isolation and loneliness which her father's money had always managed to bring her. 'Money is such a lonely word,' she added.

'Is it?' He sounded genuinely amused. 'But, in any case, it's there. Right? like the skeleton in the stinkwood cupboard.'

There were lights in the house and at various points in the extensive grounds, but Tirza knew her father was out and that Mrs Meeker and the servants would be in bed.

There was tension building up in the car and she

was aware of the woody fragrance of his after-shave lotion. With an upward tilt of her green eyes she said, 'Would you like some coffee—or a drink, maybe? It's up to you.'

'I could use a cup of coffee. As a matter of fact, I haven't been home yet. I went to the Holiday Inn with a business associate straight from my office.'

'Well, fine.' She felt flustered. She wondered whether he was testing her. 'I make very good coffee, as it so happens.' When she reached for the door catch he leaned over her and undid it for her.

The style of the house was of the Dutch architecture of Cape Town and its walls glimmered softly in the night. There were six gables, each with a graceful scroll pattern. Full-blown roses circled white columns in the garden and rosebuds unfurled their petals and their perfume mingled with hers.

At the big door Tirza fumbled in her bag for her key and when she found it Hugo Harrington took it from her. A stubborn streak in her prompted her to say, 'No, there's a knack. You won't be able to manage it.'

When she dropped the key, they both reached down for it at the same time, and her tawny hair brushed his cheek as their fingers met. When they straightened up he put the key into the lock and unlocked the massive door without any effort at all. Their eyes met and she felt a rush of something like excitement, mingled with fright.

The wide hall had a white marble floor and, above it, an enormous chandelier of Baccarat crystal sent a glitter of colour in its direction. 'This

way,' she said, leading the way into the vast drawing-room. Hugo Harrington was surprised and
showed it, just as she had known he would.
Everybody who ever came to the mansion was.

Here, there were no Cape heirlooms, no copper
warming pans and kettles, no Delftware or oil
paintings of ancestors staring down from gilt
frames. Although Douglas Harper had inherited
money from his father, to set him on the way, he
had inherited nothing else. No family tree spread
its branches to remind one of the part they had
played in Cape history. His ancestors had been
wanderers, taking root in foreign countries, only
to tear them up again and move on. Douglas
Harper was a self-made man, using his inheritance
as the first stepping-stone.

So far as the architecture was concerned the style
was Cape, but it ended there. The drawing-room
was furnished with heavy-scaled sofas and chairs,
upholstered in fantastic cream Portuguese carpeting. Her father had fallen in love with the
Portuguese carpeting when they had been visiting
Howard in Portugal. The huge area-carpet was the
same and contrasted excitingly with the honey-gold
beamed ceiling. Two palm-stump tables were used
as pedestals for wine-storing jars of tin-glazed ear-
thenware (majolica) Italian, Tuscany, late sixteenth
century. In the deep window recesses there were
more jars—Chinese wine-storing jars, which had
been made in 1850, or thereabouts. The tremendous fireplace was white. Near one of the sofas a
chunk of malachite rested on a white marble-
topped table and the shade of green accentuated

all that cream carpeting, as it had been intended it should do. White irises and giant lilies had been arranged in a vase by Tirza that morning.

'Immense and theatrical, almost—this is no ordinary room,' Hugo Harrington was saying. 'It's an exciting room, for an exciting slim girl with tawny hair the colour of the beams and green eyes the colour of that great hunk of malachite over there. The decor must have revolved around that girl from the beginning, surely?'

'This is mood furniture,' she told him. 'My father is into it.' She gave him a grin. 'Here, in this house, there are no ancestral faces frowning down at one from heavy and ornate frames. Thank goodness for *that* small mercy, anyway.' She heard the childish bitterness in her own voice. Often alone, the eyes of ancestors, trailing her about from ornate frames, would serve to make her nervous and jumpy, but she did not tell him this. Without thinking she went on, 'The only hint at tradition is in my bedroom.' She saw her mistake immediately and realised that he was still not sure of her, but she went on. 'There are exquisite blue-and-white Delft tiles inside a rather lovely white fireplace. To do away with tradition, however, there's a sunken marble bath, the size of a swimming-pool.'

'What am I supposed to say, Tirza? That I'd like to see them some time?' There was a cool expression in his eyes, although his tone was mocking. She was aware of his tallness and his tanned skin, which made those dark blue eyes seem even darker. He had a sensual mouth, but his chin was round and stubborn-looking.

'What did you get out of saying that?' she asked angrily. She felt herself begin to shake. There were two lamps burning and the light from them exploded the tiny gold flecks in her green eyes and the blue-upon-blue in his.

'You have a lot to learn about men,' he said.

'It was a brutal remark,' she replied angrily. 'Please sit down while I get the coffee.'

They were drinking it when the cream and gold telephone in the hall began screaming to be picked up. She knew that Hugo Harrington was watching her as she went through to answer it.

'Tirza?' It was her father. 'You at home, then?'

'Yes. Can't you hear I am?' From where she was standing she could see Hugo Harrington pretending to examine the green chunk of malachite. She was very pale and she touched her face with the fingers of her free hand.

'I'll be with you in, say,' she knew that her father was looking at his wrist watch, 'say, just under an hour. Sorry I missed dinner—meeting finished late. They always do.'

'That's all right, D.H. I ate alone and then I went out.'

Slowly, to give herself the time she needed, Tirza replaced the receiver and went back to the drawing-room.

'That was my father,' she said, 'in case you wondered.'

Turning, he said, 'What I can't understand is why you have to model? It's obvious that you live in a world of money and security and, no doubt, with no thought of tomorrow.'

'I don't have to model. I model because I want to.' Her tone was brusque.

'I'll take your word for it.' His eyes were on her face. 'And to think I was going to offer you a job!'

'What kind of job?'

'I have this weaving industry in Swaziland ... it's called the Swazi Signature Weaving Industry. There's a boutique in Cape Town and another in Swaziland. I have a partner, by the way. He sees to the Swaziland side of things—mostly, anyway. I often have to go there. We often employ girls to model our fashion lines.'

'Are you still going to offer me this job?' she asked.

'I think it's a logical conclusion that I'm not.' He glanced around. 'You have here a very swish address.'

'I don't see that makes any difference.'

'Then you're interested?'

After a moment she said, 'It isn't an easy decision to make at a moment's notice, is it? I'd have to think about it.'

'I'll ring you,' he said. 'Where do I find you in the directory?'

'I'll write it down,' she told him. She got tired of people exclaiming 'Are you Douglas Harper's daughter, then?'

Next to the telephone number she wrote, Tirza.

When she handed him the small white card he glanced up at her, 'Tirza?'

'Mrs Meeker will probably answer,' she told him, and sounded suddenly tired and impatient. 'Now, if you don't mind ... I'm terribly tired.'

'All right,' he said, 'let's not argue about it.'

Her eyes followed him moodily as he went out-side to where his Alfa-Romeo was parked beneath the white pillars with the twining pink and yellow roses. She heard the engine start, and then the lights came on. As he drove past the wide steps he tooted twice.

In her room, with the white fireplace and blue-and-white Delft tiles, she cried a little, feeling bruised and bewildered—but not much, for she had made the discovery, a long time ago, that tears did not help. Instead, she put her head back on her pillows and her lashes went down and she allowed herself to sink into a kind of comatose state of sheer misery.

CHAPTER TWO

THE following day was blustery, but, with its thick cream rug and the dark-green ornamental tree which grew in a container placed in a huge basket to one side of the tremendous small-paned windows, Tirza's room was cool and calm.

Mrs Meeker sent coffee to her room and the maid placed it on the table, beside the bed.

'Thank you.' Tirza sat up. She was wearing a striped cotton man's shirt—one of several she liked to wear. She had gone shopping with Nigel one day, and had bought several shirts because the colours were so striking. The shop was called Do Your Own Thing.

'Sadie, please tell Mrs Meeker not to cook breakfast for me. I'm not hungry.'

She felt disinclined to face the day and sank back on her pillows thinking about Nigel Wright who had gone out of his way, with measured skill, to woo her. It all fell into pattern now, she thought bitterly . . . his dislike of crowds, always choosing those discreet little restaurants, drives which led to quiet fishing villages. A wildness came over her that a man should do this to her. What was it Hugo Harrington had said last night? You have a lot to learn about men.

Suddenly, everything about the steely, sophisticated Hugo Harrington was exaggerated in her mind, and a rage built up against him too . . . the way he had caught her looking at him and held her eyes for a long disturbing moment, before going over her briefly. The manner in which he had said, 'Do I know you?' She would, she could see, have to arm herself against this elusive quality in a galaxy of men who realised the power they had to cause women to make fools of themselves.

Restlessly, she threw back the bedclothes and stood up. She spent a long time in the bath, brooding on the past month, and was thankful that she had at least found out that Nigel was married after only one month. Things could have been worse for her. It was her friend Sandra Ballington who had said, 'I suppose you know what you're doing?'

'What do you mean?'

'Well, I've seen you about with Nigel Wright. Don't tell me you didn't *know*? He's married, Tirza.'

Men like Nigel Wright, she found herself thinking now, shouldn't marry. Men with a combination of charm and looks which could hardly fail to turn heads, including their own.

Some time later Mrs Meeker came into her room to find out whether she was feeling ill.

'I'm okay now, thanks. I—I had an upset, but I'm getting over it now,' said Tirza, moving a bowl of roses out of the sun which was streaming into the lovely room, so that Mrs Meeker would not see her face.

'What kind of upset, dear?' Mrs Meeker showed concern.

A fragile breeze in the room was laden with the

scent of roses which caused Tirza's throat to tighten.

'I just felt sick. It will pass, don't worry.' Turning, she tried to smile casually.

She was having coffee with her father the following evening when Hugo Harrington phoned.

'What do you *see* in him?' His voice was mocking. 'Don't tell me you're still moping over that character?' She could imagine him, suave and handsome, wearing well-cut trousers and a silk shirt, maybe—open at the chest.

She touched the nape of her neck. From where she was standing she could see her father in the drawing-room, with its sofas and chairs of imposing dimensions and upholstered in rich cream Portuguese carpeting.

It was difficult to believe that Hugo Harrington had been in this room. So far as she had been concerned he had been a ship that passed in the night.

'I'm surprised you remembered,' she replied stiffly. 'It's in the past now, so far as I'm concerned. You see, in a space of a short time I've reached the very comfortable stage where I don't take the opposite sex all that seriously.'

'Outwardly calm, but inwardly very tense, in other words.' He laughed softly.

'Not at all. What can I do for you? You didn't ring just to talk about this little episode in my life, surely?' Her voice was frigid.

'I said I'd ring,' he told her. 'In two days' time I'll be going off to Swaziland. We're putting on a fashion show there, at the Royal Swazi Hotel.'

'I'm not really a model,' she cut in, 'if this is what you have in mind.'

'Think,' he went on, 'you'll be getting away from it all—to the endless grasslands, those rocky hills rising towards the mountains. Lunch with me tomorrow and we'll talk about it.'

'I'll think about it,' her voie was stilted. 'Right now, I'm with someone.'

'So am I with someone, right now.' She was quick to notice the impatience in his voice. 'I'm as anxious to get back as you are. I'll pick you up tomorrow, say at . . .'

'If I come,' she told him, 'it will be on my own steam. *I* can drive.'

'Right. Say one-fifteen at the Bistro Baobab.'

She wanted to go, that was the shattering part of it. She wanted to be back in the swing of things to make her forget what a fool she had been. 'All right, but I really have to go now. I'm—er—busy.'

'Watch it,' he said, and she knew he was smiling. 'What are you trying to do to yourself—commit suicide?' He rang off.

So sure of her, she thought bitterly. Hugo Harrington was the type who would never think of losing.

When she rejoined her father she said, 'D.H., I want to work for you.'

Douglas Harper looked up from the booklet on gold shares.

'You want to work for *me*?' He sounded frankly surprised. 'What about this boutique—this . . .' he hunted around in his mind for the name—'this Lotus Flower, is it?'

'I only help out there, really. I've invested a little money in it and I model for them sometimes, but it's not what I consider to be a full-time position. Sometimes I feel so useless. D. H., I want you to take me into the business.'

'What is it you want to do?' he asked.

'I want to be one of your buyers. I want to start off by going to Swaziland on a buying spree for Harper's.'

He infuriated her by laughing outright. 'You want to be a buyer? But, my dear girl, I already have buyers, more than I damn well know what to do with, if it comes to that.'

'Look,' she said, 'it's terribly important to me. I'm twenty-three, right? I'm getting exactly nowhere, right? I'll tell you what I want to do. There's this weaving industry in Swaziland and, because I want to get away for a while, I want to go there first. While I'm there, I want to see for myself what goes on. I'm more than just a little interested, as it so happens.'

'What do you intend buying from these people?' he asked, but she could see that he was beginning to fidget, as his mind strayed to the booklet which he was still holding.

'Mohair fabrics, to be made up into curtaining, wall-hangings and couture garments for Harper's.'

'There's nothing new there,' he said.

'Perhaps not, but there might be something different. In any case, apart from buying I want to start my own weaving industry at the farm in the Karroo.'

'Well,' her father sounded surprised, 'this is a

new one on me, Tirza. What do you think you
know about weaving?'

'Only a little. But I want to have a look and
work out whether I have it in me to start a small
industry—without any help from you.'

'I see.' He fingered his chin.

'You're always moaning about Howard,' Tirza
went on, trying to keep her mind from the music
coming from the expensive stereo. The words
hammered at her brain . . . Honey, I'm lost without
you. I'm really going to have to do something,
without *you* in my life . . .

Sadie, the maid with the coppery skin, came in
for the white-and-ginger Beit-Hayotser coffee cups.
The soft hair framing Sadie's face looked like soft
teased-out mohair, Tirza found herself thinking.

Douglas Harper took this moment to get back
to his facts and figures on gold shares, and Tirza
stared resentfully at him. 'Well?' she said, finally.

'I'll have to think about it,' he answered.

In the struggle to hold on to her temper Tirza
gazed about the beautiful room which, because of
the architectural style of the house, should have
been furnished in the traditional Cape-style
manner, but wasn't. At the time of decorating, after
the house had been completed, her father had
called in an interior decorator. Even then, she
seethed, she had been given no role to play.
Douglas Harper had told the decorator to 'come
up with something unique—give the house freedom'. What was it he had said, 'I have no traditional heirlooms I want to display.' Nothing, except
his daughter!

'D.H.,' her voice sounded loud, even to her own ears, 'I'm trying to discuss something with you. Will you please *listen*? I want to be a buyer and I want to leave for Swaziland almost immediately. I want to get away.'

'Is this your only reason for wanting to be a buyer?' He sounded impatient now.

'I want to strike while the iron is hot,' she said, after a moment. 'Before I change my mind. I don't want to go on in this useless fashion. If I don't go to Swaziland now I might never go and, in turn, I might never start that weaving industry.'

'Where will you stay?' he surprised her by asking.

'What difference does it make?' She shrugged her shoulders.

'You've never been to Swaziland,' he pointed out.

'No, but I know enough. There's the Ezulwini Holiday Inn. There's the Royal Swazi Spa—any one of those . . .'

'I don't like that.' He threw the blue and gold booklet on the bush-hammered travertine top of the low coffee table. His black eyebrows were beginning to bush. 'If I agree to this scheme of yours,' he said, after a moment, 'it will be on the understanding that you'll stay with Cathy Mobray, if she'll have you.'

'*If* you agree!' She was angry now. 'D.H., isn't it just about time you began to realise that I'm over twenty-one? And, by the way, who is Cathy Mobray?' When he made no reply she found herself saying, 'Perhaps it was a love affair?'

'I wouldn't say that,' he took a breath. 'The only

woman I ever really loved was your mother. But Cathy is a woman I very nearly married—some time ago.'

'How long ago?'

'When I was busy with the farm,' he said quietly.

That was when he had bought the farm, with the house on it, Tirza thought, and the adjoining land with the country hotel on it, which had been converted into the most magnificent homestead.

'You didn't tell me.' Her voice was abrupt.

'Well, I'm telling you now. What difference does it make?' He reacted impatiently.

'Better late than never,' she said, still in that same abrupt voice. 'At least, so they say.'

'Actually, I bought the Karroo farm, and the adjoining hotel, because of Cathy,' he went on. 'That's why I had the hotel converted. I thought we could all stay there, you know ... that I'd make it my headquarters, as it were, operate my affairs from there, apart from those times when I have to travel, of course.'

'Who is *all*?' she asked, her eyes on his face.

'Cathy has a daughter. Her name is Paige.'

Tirza felt resentment building up. 'There was Cathy and Cathy has a daughter. I wondered at the time just why you bought that farm, and you never did get around to telling me. What happened? Between you, I mean?'

'Oh,' he shrugged, 'she changed her mind. More or less at the last moment.'

'After you'd had the hotel converted and the interior decorator had finished she just changed her

A New Look for Harlequin Romance

Introducing a new cover
design for the most
popular romance series in
history. This new design
brings a fresh bright look
for spring.

The new design debuts
with our March
publications.

mind? And you want me to stay with a woman like that?' Her voice was heated.

'Apart from that, I suppose we were both to blame. Cathy is . . .'

Tirza cut in, 'Cathy Mobray changed her mind, more or less at the last moment, and yet all the time I knew nothing about what was going on. Tell me, was Paige, Cathy's daughter, kept in the dark? It would be interesting to know, D.H.'

'You would have been told, in time.' He was beginning to sound irritable again. 'Look, Tirza, let me get in touch with Cathy.'

'I don't want to stay with this woman.' She stood up and went across to the chunk of malachite. Trailing her fingers over its surface, she glanced angrily at her father.

'Well, it's a stipulation I have to make, like it or not. If you're going to Swaziland on your own, to buy, you will stay with somebody I know. Take it or leave it. It's your choice.'

'You're an impossible man,' she said crossly. 'You don't ever seem to mind when you leave me here alone while you go off to a different country.'

'That's different. You're left behind in good hands, and in your own home.'

'Won't you change your mind?' she asked. 'I'll be perfectly all right in a hotel.'

'You will stay in a private home, or not at all.'

'Okay,' she said on a hard little breath. 'If that's how you want it.'

She tried to conceal her surprise when her father tapped on her door some time later. 'I've been in touch with Cathy,' he told her, getting to the point.

'You'll be very welcome to stay there. I won't pretend that I'm in favour of all this—I'm not. Anyway, before you leave I'll arrange a meeting with Werner, in my office. He'll put you wise about one or two things. He does our buying in Lesotho.'

'Thank you,' she said. 'You see, I really want to go.'

'By the way, I merely told Cathy that you were one of our buyers.'

'Fine.' Tirza felt a stab of apprehension and bit her lip.

The following day she drove into town and met Hugo Harrington at the Bistro Baobab. The atmosphere of the bistro was decidedly casual and lunch was already in full swing. Massed poppies were arranged everywhere and the striped tan-and-white awnings had been lowered, against the sun, at all the arched windows.

They were shown to their table and were immediately involved in choosing partridge with a garnish of button onions and bacon rolls which would be served with buttered peas and new potatoes and a good wine to go with it. Without realising it, Tirza had the unconscious grace that stems from the kind of expensive life her father had provided for her, but now that all the preliminaries were over she looked across the round table at Hugo Harrington and her green eyes were wide and worried. He was taller than she remembered, she found herself thinking, as she met the full force of his dark blue eyes.

'I really don't know why I'm here,' she told him.

'I am, quite possibly, not going to model for you.'

He leaned indolently back in his chair. 'Nevertheless, in a mood of self-searching and indecision, you decided to have lunch with me, is that it?'

'I was being tactful when I agreed. You see, I was in the middle of having coffee after dinner, and I wanted to get back,' she explained.

'In other words, you were with a man?' He glanced idly round the restaurant and then returned to lock his eyes with hers.

'Yes.' She did not tell him that the man in question was her father.

'So he came back?' He went on regarding her.

'No.'

'I was right, then. So you rustled up someone else?' He was watching her with lazy scorn.

'I've known him a long time.' She hoped he did not hear her small unsettled intake of breath. 'But all this is beside the point, don't you think? I didn't agree to have lunch with you to discuss my private life, after all.'

'Fine. So let's get down to business. It's a logical conclusion, Tirza, that you do in fact have modelling at the back of your mind. Right?'

'Well, I'll be honest. I'm interested in what you have to tell me.'

Their food arrived at that particular moment and then when they were settled Hugo said, 'After Swaziland we have permission to put on a fashion show in the Game Park. We've never done this before. It's a breakthrough to promote our garments. At the same time, I'll be combining this with work I usually do on these visits. This work revolves around supplying the curio shops in the Park with our goods.'

'I see. How many girls will be going to the Game Reserve, by the way?' Tirza wished he would let up on his scrutiny of her.

'Two. You and one other girl, plus a wardrobe mistress. As a matter of fact, these two women run our boutique in Mbabane.'

After a moment she said, 'The way you spoke, I imagined a whole . . . fleet of models.'

'Does that worry you? In any case, there'll be four girls, five with you, participating in our show at the Royal Swazi Hotel. This amount is to be whittled down to two models for the Game Park. And by the way, we fly from Cape Town to Swaziland to meet up with the others. That's how I commute between our business there and in Cape Town. So that long intimate drive, which might just be bothering you at the back of your mind, is non-existent . . . unfortunately.'

Slim and glamorous, with careful make-up, Tirza chose to ignore his remark.

'But,' he went on, 'we'll travel together on the flight.' His dark blue eyes fenced with herrs and she felt the vitality of him. He was wearing well-cut dark trousers and a white silk shirt and she was aware of the disturbing glimpse of his tanned skin between his shirt where he had left the buttons undone. A gold chain and medallion gleamed between the dark hairs on his chest when he moved. There was, she thought, an arrestingly hard, masculine beauty about him. In fact, he looked almost piratical.

Turning away from him, she made a big thing of looking at the view. From where their table was situated they could see the winding streets, beyond the sun-awnings, and glimpses of Table Mountain. Before entering the bistro she had noticed that the breeze seemed to carry with it spicy and fruity scents, mingled with sweet and sour and the flowers that blazed in tins of water at the flower sellers nearby.

When she lifted her glass it was with a hand that shook slightly. Looking across at Hugo, she saw that he had been about to drink from his glass and was aware of his quick, considering look over her body and then they drank slowly, their eyes on each other.

'I really can't make up my mind,' she told him, after a moment. 'I'll be honest with you, I *do* have to go to Swaziland on business, though.'

'Then let me make up your mind for you.' His smile held sardonic amusement, but his blue eyes were watchful, she felt.

'No, give me tonight to think it over,' she murmured.

'You wanted this opportunity to get to know me better, is that it?' He smiled faintly. 'You're more cautious than I believed, Tirza. And by the way, you never did tell me ... Tirza who?'

'Models are usually known only by their first names,' she replied in her most expressionless voice. 'You should know that.'

'What's the mystery?' he asked abruptly.

'There is no mystery, but in any case,' she made

up her mind on the spur of the moment, 'my name is Tirza Theron.' It was not altogether a lie, she consoled herself. She had been christened Tirza Theron Harper, after her mother.

'Who do you usually model for?' he asked.

'*When* I model, you mean?' She gave him a casual smile. 'Oh,' she shrugged, 'I have a few irons in the fire. It's too complicated, really . . .'

'What kind of dumb answer is that, Tirza Theron?'

'Well, a boutique called Lotus Flower, if that means anything.'

She saw that he was trying, very hard, not to be irritable, and she felt her heart begin to accelerate. Her game of deceit was beginning to unnerve her already. It was, she knew, absurd to feel so hung up about being Douglas Harper's daughter . . . *the* Douglas Harper of Harper's.

'In other words,' Hugo reached again for his glass, openly going over her face and shoulders with his blue eyes, 'you do just enough to make life interesting.'

'For someone who's only known me a short time, you certainly form a lot of opinions, don't you?' There was an edge to her voice.

'You seem to forget, I'm your future employer. I've got to be sure about these things.' He had a way of turning a situation to his own advantage, she thought, looking into his mocking eyes.

'Oh, quite.' Her voice was very cool.

'And you dressed to please me, right?' He gave her a brief smile and then glanced into his drink.

'Really? What makes you think that?'

'Your skin is carefully made up, your tawny blonde hair luxuriant and left to cascade those slim shoulders, nails beautifully manicured and polished. Those dreamy green eyes were shaded by oversize sunglasses, when we met outside the restaurant, just to create enough mystery.' He reached for his glass again and held it with his fingertips around the rim, and went on studying her. The expression in his eyes seemed darker as he made his calculations about her.

'Perhaps I should have worn a plain black sweater—and twelve rows of pearls?' There was a degree of annoyance in her voice.

'Well,' he smiled, 'they are coming back into fashion, after all—pearls, sweaters, sequins, padded shoulders. Your mother probably wore them.'

'I didn't know my mother,' she said stiffly. 'She died in India when I was little.'

'I see.' She saw his eyes flicker. 'Well, to get back to business. Your mouth is too wide, of course, your green eyes too large for that bronze face of yours but, somehow, together, they have an incredible effect. You'll do.'

'I need the work,' she told him. 'For this reason I have put up with your bantering and, for this reason, I'm going to accept your offer.'

'You can't seriously expect me to believe that!' Hugo sat back and regarded her. 'Just be honest and say that what you do need is to get away for a while, and I've traded on this.'

'Why?'

'Because you have the right statistics and I want this show in Swaziland—and in the Game Reserve, for that matter—to be a success. It's as simple as that.'

'In other words, you're using me because of what you saw and heard the other night at the Holiday Inn, is that it?'

'Yes. And let's face this—*you* are using *me*.' His gaze locked momentarily with hers.

For a while Tirza remained aloof and listened to him while he spoke about modelling fees and what would be expected of her.

Later, she said, 'I'll fly up on my own. I have one or two things to settle before I leave Cape Town. I'll leave a day after you.' She watched him as he took a sip of his wine and listened to her without any change of expression and then he said,

'Fine. In this case, Tirza, you will sign a contract before I leave for Swaziland.'

She could feel the beating of her heart. 'Why?'

'You must be joking,' he laughed shortly. 'I plan ahead. To make sure you get there.'

'Contracts are made to be broken.' She regarded him with new eyes.

'Not my contracts. And you'd do well to remember this, Miss Theron.'

After lunch they went to the offices of his Cape Town branch and when she had signed the necessary contract Hugo said, 'I'm pinning you down. This must be upsetting for you.' He stared deeply into her eyes and the tone of his voice was slightly sarcastic.

'Not at all.' Tirza struggled to keep her temper under control. 'I find the contract businesslike and in order.'

On the other hand, she was aware of a complete sense of freedom ... freedom from everything which had gone to make up her shortlived romance with Nigel Wright.

When they parted he touched her with his eyes. 'I'll meet your plane in Swaziland,' he said, for she had already reserved a seat on the plane from his office, using the name she had used on the contract—Tirza Theron.

'That won't be necessary,' she told him, making up her mind on the spur of the moment. 'You see, I'm being met by a friend. I'll be staying with her, in fact. I'll contact you immediately upon my arrival.'

For a moment their eyes held. 'I'll be expecting you, Tirza Theron.'

CHAPTER THREE

SHE arrived in Swaziland in sweltering heat and looked around for Cathy Mobray who had arranged, on the phone, with her father to meet her.

'You're Tirza, of course, and you look just like your father.'

Turning, Tirza said, 'Oh, hello. You must be Mrs Mobray.' She laughed shyly.

On the way to the car Cathy said, 'Please call me Cathy—everybody does. I'd feel so old, otherwise. You see, I always seem to mix with young people.' Although she had spoken almost carelessly, Tirza had the feeling that Cathy Mobray was feeling more than just a little tense at meeting Douglas Harper's daughter. 'Paige is at work, of course,' she went on. 'We both help run a boutique in Mbabane.'

'Really? Birds of a feather, then,' Tirza smiled.

A flicker of interest and surprise crossed Cathy's face. 'Don't tell me that's what *you* do, Tirza? I mean, you don't have to work, surely?'

'I have an interest in a small boutique. My real work is that of buyer for Harper's.'

'Yes, your father told me that part of it.'

'It's to be a case of killing two birds with one stone, as he often says,' Tirza laughed lightly, in an effort to feel more relaxed with this woman.

'I'm to do a spot of modelling while I'm in Swaziland. Into the bargain, I'm doing a bit of scouting around. You see, I intend opening a weaving industry in the not so distant future, thus putting the farm in the Karroo to further use.'

'And so it's really killing three birds with one stone,' Cathy replied. 'I'm really curious about all this. You must tell me more when we get home.'

Cathy Mobray's house was calm and peaceful and had a spectacular view of the Ezulwini Valley, surrounded by the majestic Mudzimba range. Ivy and petria trailed down the pillars of the wide, spacious veranda.

Dark, stormy clouds had gathered above the mountains and it looked as though a storm was about to break and rain would put out the mountain fires which were sending up swirls of dark grey smoke, in various areas.

They went into the house, which had high, thatched ceilings, and Tirza's eyes immediately went to the mohair curtains, muted striped mohair upholstery on the long sofas and chairs, mohair wall-hangings and off-white carpet which, no doubt, all came from the Swazi Signature Weaving Industry.

Thunder rumbled menacingly on the mountaintops surrounding the Ezulwini Valley and the windows of the house rattled faintly.

'You've arrived just in time,' said Cathy. 'There's going to be a terrible storm, by the looks of things.'

'Thank you for putting me up ... Cathy,' Tirza used the name with difficulty. 'It's very kind of you.'

'You're most welcome. I'll hustle tea up, or coffee, Tirza. Which do you prefer? Anyway, let me show you to your room first.'

Feeling slightly embarrassed, Tirza followed the woman her father had nearly married, wondering what had gone wrong with the romance.

The room had dusky-blue walls and more hand-woven work—a pure new wool and mohair bouclé-weave bedcover, fine golden mohair curtains and an off-white carpet. Against the pale blue and cream the rich honey-coloured curtains, thatched ceiling and supporting wooden beams looked superb. After a moment Tirza ventured to say, 'What a beautiful room. At a guess I would say you patronise the Swazi Signature. Do you, Cathy?'

'Why, yes.' Cathy's dark eyes scanned the room. 'Everything you see in this house comes from there. Is this where you have come to buy?'

'I'm hoping to place an order. By the way, Cathy, I'm also doing a stint of modelling, while I'm in Swaziland. I didn't mention this to my father, though—he worries so. In fact, one of his stipulations was that I should stay with you, if you would have me, of course.'

'Nothing gives me more pleasure,' murmured Cathy.

'By the way, how far is the Swazi Signature from here?' Tirza felt her face grow warm.

'Next door, practically, as the crow flies.' Cathy laughed lightly, but there was an edge to the sound. 'Let's get something straight, Tirza. You'll be buying from Hugo Harrington and you'll be modelling for him. Is that right?'

Suddenly Tirza's muscles tensed. 'Do you know him, then—Hugo Harrington?'

'Do I know him? I should do. He treats this place almost as a second home, when he's in Swaziland. How well do you know him?' The words sounded coldly polite.

'Not very well.' Tirza's mind was busy with the way in which she had deceived Hugo by telling him that her surname was Theron and the blunder she had made by telling Cathy that she was scouting— that was the damaging word—around in view of the fact that she intended starting a weaving industry. 'Just on a business level, really.'

'I see. Well, settle in, then, and—what would you like, tea or coffee?'

'Tea will be lovely, thank you, Cathy.'

Hugo Harrington, Tirza thought worriedly, after Cathy had left the room, had an assortment of opinions about her already. What was he going to think when he discovered that she had lied to him about her name? What would he think when he learned that she intended going into business on her own, after having used the Swazi Signature as a kind of stepping-stone for ideas and know-how?

Over tea, Cathy said, 'Talking about the Swazi Signature, you must know, of course, that Hugo started the weaving industry—which is already world renowned, I might go so far as to add.'

Cathy was slim and tanned and not very tall, and elegant in a white skirt and a black top which had a wide collar, turned up, against the edge of her dark hair, which had silver threads in it.

'I didn't know, actually.' Tirza felt strangely depressed now.

'What's more,' Cathy went on, 'Paige, who runs his Mbabane boutique, is also modelling at the Royal Swazi Hotel. I'm—well, wardrobe mistress.'

'It's a small world,' Tirza's voice sounded forced, even to her own ears. 'Isn't it?'

'Not really. We just all happen to be moving in the same circles, I suppose,' Cathy replied abruptly.

'Have you seen him, by the way, since he got back?' Tirza asked. 'I mean, has he found out that I'll be staying here with you?'

'I didn't know he was back.' Cathy sounded frankly peeved at this piece of news.

'I arranged to phone him directly I arrived in Swaziland. Being in the country like this, Cathy, I don't suppose there's a bus service? I mean, I could take a joyride,' Tirza found herself beginning to flounder, 'and announce myself.'

'I'll drive you there if you like, although there's going to be a storm,' said Cathy, and the knot of tension pulled tighter.

'Oh, no, Cathy, I wasn't hinting . . .'

'I know you weren't—but look, take the car yourself. It's not far once you get on to the main road and continue until you see the signpost on the left-hand side of the road. I'd overlooked the fact that a friend is dropping in this afternoon to collect a parcel.'

Cathy, Tirza thought, seemed eager to get rid of her.

'It seems an awful nerve, on my part,' she felt compelled to say, but nevertheless she knew an urgency to explain things to Hugo Harrington before he got the story second-hand.

'Fine, if you're not afraid of storms?' Cathy surveyed her with an unfathomable expression.

'No, I'm not, as it happens.'

'Well then, that's settled . . . take a drive out there. You can't miss it.'

The storm had broken by the time Tirza reached the weaving settlement. In fact, she thought, the weather seemed to have gone insane, all of a sudden—like this whole venture.

She asked for Hugo Harrington and was told that he was at the studio, and directed there. The studio was only a short distance away from the settlement, but it was necessary to drive there.

Getting out of the car, finally, she ran through the drenching rain in the direction of the studio. He was there, looking just as she remembered him, only much, much better, and she felt a sudden exhilaration at the discovery.

Two Swazi maidens, in traditional colourful Swazi garb, featuring orange-red print toga-like garments—the *mahiya*—and beehive hairstyles, stood stirring bubbling cauldrons, in the Macbeth style, of aniline dyes, which would take a new load of mohair. Even while they were working, there was a radiant look about each girl which suggested the singing and rhythmic dancing which was so much a part of the country of spectacular views, cool mountain streams and almost every other example of African landscape.

To the full orchestration of rain and thunder, lightning played along the looms, at the far end of the white-walled, thatched studio. For a moment, Hugo's dark blue eyes didn't seem to focus properly when he saw Tirza standing there, with the storm raging behind the square opening to the building, her fabulous tawny hair wild and free. In the peculiar light of the storm her scarlet silk shirt seemed very bright and accentuated her grape-green eyes. Her perfume pervaded the room.

'Hello,' she said nervously. 'Remember me?'

'What are you doing here?' His eyes went over her damp clothes. 'You were going to phone me from your friend's home.'

'I decided to drive out here instead.'

'Looking at you, standing there,' he said, 'I know I've seen you before.'

'Let me fill you in,' she tried to sound flippant. 'On the Eastern Boulevard, Cape Town. Now, do you remember?'

'You've appeared in magazines,' he went on, 'newspapers . . .'

'Well, of course. Models often do.' Her heart was racing. 'Tell me, I have come to the right place? This is the Swazi Signature Weaving Industry?'

There was a terrific flash of lightning, followed by a loud explosion of thunder. The Swazi girls shrieked and Hugo said, 'Why don't you come *right in*, damn it, out of the storm, Tirza.'

'I was waiting to be invited. In any case,' to hide her nervousness she continued to be flighty, 'I have waterproof make-up which is immune to rain and tears.'

'Well, unless you happen to carry your own lightning conductor around with you, come in.'

Shaking back her hair, she said, 'I'm not afraid of storms. I'm *excited* by them. I enjoy nature's pyrotechnics.'

She was aware that the white denim jeans she was wearing were damp and that her scarlet shirt was clinging to her bosom.

The rain, gathering over the mountains, swept towards the opening to the building in fierce squalls of wind. 'A stormy start to our contract,' said Hugo. In an abrupt yet not ungraceful movement, he took her by the shoulders and drew her right into the building, which was without a door. She saw that his skin glowed dark and tanned. He was wearing jeans and a blue cotton shirt, open at the neck. The sensation his fingers had caused to surge through her, as he had drawn her right in out of the rain, flustered her, and the steady drumming of the rain on the paved area outside sounded very loud. They stood like this for a brief moment, then he dropped his arms to his sides while Tirza brushed her damp hair from her face.

'You haven't told me why you're here. Is there some kind of snag?' he asked.

'No snag,' she went on dragging her damp hair through her fingers, shaking it back from her face.

His eyes went past her. 'You were supposed to fly. How come the car?'

Tirza's cloud of apprehension grew. 'It belongs to my friend. Soon after my arrival in Swaziland, I found out that you know her . . . Cathy Mobray.'

A sudden change came over his face and she felt

that he was aware of the fact that, despite her outward self-assurance, she was unsure of herself.

'It never occurred to me that you might know
her,' he said, 'but you know what they say, it's a
small world. So you borrowed Cathy's car and
came all the way out here, in a raging storm, just
to tell me that you've arrived?' This appeared to
intrigue him. 'I have learned one thing about you,
and that is you can be pretty silly at times.'

The women at the looms were packing up now,
preparing to leave. A mini-bus had pulled up outside. Suddenly, lightning struck nearby, possibly a
tall tree, and although Tirza's teeth went down on
her lip she did not even blink. The thunder which
followed almost immediately was almost deafening,
but Hugo remained unmoved. He was not the type
of man who would be the victim of any kind of
situation ... he would always be the conqueror
and, what was more, he would not take kindly to
any form of deceit, whether it concerned his love-
life or his business.

As she stood there watching him, she was aware
of her clothing and the way in which her damp
shirt was clinging to her bosom. Her mind flitted
to the fragile lacy tanga-briefs and bra she was
wearing, for his eyes had passed over her again,
and she put one tanned arm across her chest and
held her other arm with tense fingers. She had been
shocked at the expression in those dark blue eyes,
behind their thick black lashes.

'You'd better get back and change,' he said, 'as
soon as the rain lifts a little.'

Outside, however, the rain was still hissing and

pelting down, while lightning continued to dart
round the white-walled studio, lighting up everything. Hugo glanced at his watch. 'I was about to
leave here, as a matter of fact. The women have
been doing shift-work. We're working on a change-
over scheme. The office is closed already, and so is
the showroom. This is what we call the studio.'

'I know. They told me back there, when I asked
for you. They told me you'd be here.'

'Was there something special you wanted to see
me about?' His voice and manner had authority.

'Well, no, not really.' The noisy confusion of the
storm and the fact that she did not know how to
prepare him for what Cathy Mobray might have
to tell him about the real reason of her visit to
Swaziland caused her to swallow. 'I'm . . .' she
broke off and glanced around the room, 'interested
in weaving, you know.'

'You're interested in weaving, but you don't
weave. I remember, we discussed this over a drink
on the Eastern Boulevard. You said you merely
had a knowledge of looms—*and things*,' he added,
with unveiled mockery.

'Well, I often model garments which are made
from superfine mohair, after all.' Somehow she
couldn't tell him that her real name was Harper
and not Theron and that she was interested in the
weaving industry for the very simple reason that
she wanted to start her own business. What she
wanted, really, was to obliterate this whole
wretched visit to Swaziland . . . to undo all that
she had told Cathy. But it was too late.

'I can't show you around now. Perhaps another

time.' His male superiority aggravated her and she felt snubbed and tried to hide it by saying, 'Do you live near here? Near to your work?'

'I have a cottage, which I use when I'm here. It's not very far away—quite near to the Mobrays, in fact. I'll have to show you some time.' His eyes lingered on hers a second too long to be indifferent.

Glancing at the square opening, Tirza said, 'Well, the rain seems to have lifted, even if just a little. I must go.'

Hugo went out into the rain with her and when they were next to Cathy's car he said, 'I'll be in touch.' The smell of drenched eucalyptus trees was strong in the hissing air. One of the trees had been stripped of its bark, and several branches lay upon the ground. The tree had a burnt look about it.

'It's been struck, hasn't it?' Tirza had to raise her voice over the rain and thunder.

'You shouldn't have come out. Couldn't you see there was going to be a storm?' His eyes rested on her mouth and it was almost as if she could feel the pressure of his lips on hers. He opened the door for her and she brushed against him as she slipped into the seat. When she looked up at him, the truth exploded in her. She was more than just a little attracted to Hugo Harrington.

She put the car into reverse and began to move, then she swung the car round and drove back down the rainswept hill.

Cathy Mobray's thatched bungalow dripped in the pelting rain. Tirza parked the car in one of the open garages. In a lawned courtyard, around which the house was built, a beautiful erythremia tree was moving in the wind and shaking off the rain from its leaves and branches. In the sombre light, the branches appeared almost black. The atmosphere was rustic but beautifully elegant, thought Tirza.

Directly she got to the door she slipped her feet out of her wet sandals and then she went into the long, exciting lounge which led directly off the veranda.

The mohair upholstery, curtains and carpeting served as a reminder of why she had decided to come here, in the first place ... which was to feel her way in getting a weaving industry together on her father's farm in the Karroo.

After the fury of the rain outside, everything in here seemed quiet. It was difficult to believe, when she looked up at that golden thatch, which rose up in angles like the roof of a church, that the elements had gone wild. In a corner, next to the honey-hued curtains, there was an arrangement of carefully prepared and dried bougainvillaea, in shades of bronze and powdery mauve.

Cathy came through from one of the other rooms and crossed over to turn on the golden-shaded lamps. 'It's quite dark now,' she said conversationally, as she moved about the room, 'because of this deluge. What a storm! Well,' she swung round suddenly, taking Tirza by surprise, 'how did things go up there?'

Suddenly Tirza was aware that there was a game to play, for some unknown reason. Cathy had an angry look in her dark eyes, even though her voice was mild enough.

'Oh, fine. I just let him know that one of his

models,' she broke off as Cathy cut in sweetly, 'and his buyer,' and then continued, feeling at a distinct disadvantage now, 'had arrived.'

'You're a remarkable girl, Tirza.' It was humiliating to have Cathy look at her like that.

'So are you, Cathy. Tell me, what *did* happen between you and my father? Why did you break it off—and at the last moment, too?'

'Well, since you've succeeded in changing the subject, my dear girl, I just couldn't go through with it.' Cathy lifted her shoulders and allowed them to drop. 'I may live way out in the country, to all outward appearances, but it's easy to get around here. I have my friends in Swaziland, the casinos, the boutique. The idea of living in the semi-desert Karroo suddenly turned me off. Also, I had Paige to think of. She would have gone mad, because she would have come with me, of course.'

'I see.'

'By the way,' Cathy went on, still in that same hard voice, 'Hugo Harrington will be dining here this evening.' She kept her eyes on Tirza, obviously waiting for her reaction. 'I've just telephoned him.'

A cold, sobering shock ran through Tirza and after a little pause she said, taking advantage of the situation, 'Oh, he didn't tell me. Anyway, the fact that I've already seen him does away with those tedious introductions, doesn't it?'

The strain of trying to say all the right things was already beginning to tell on her and she was plunged into depression.

'I think I'd better go and change, Cathy.'

'Yes, you do that, darling.' Cathy's smile did not reach her eyes.

CHAPTER FOUR

PAIGE MOBRAY was tanned and blonde, unlike her mother, but shared her lack of inches.

'I was surprised to hear you knew one another.' Paige was regarding Hugo Harrington with something like distrust and disappointment, and Tirza, watching them all, could feel her pulse quicken.

'You're thinking, of course, that perhaps it was a love affair.' Hugo's voice was level, though the mockery in it was pronounced. Looking across at Cathy, he said, 'Here, let me do that for you.' He went over to Cathy, who was busy at a tall yellow-wood drinks cabinet next to the windows where the dried bougainvillaea glowed richly against the white wall and gold mohair curtaining.

'Well,' Paige went on, 'if you don't tell me, my imagination will get to work, won't it?' Her voice sounded forced, and so did the light laugh that followed the question.

'Oh, come,' Hugo retorted in a careless way, 'you should know better than to ask.'

The storm had passed over, but the lawns were saturated and soggy outside. A moon raced through wisps of silver and black cloud and it was much cooler.

Hugo was obviously very much at home in the Mobray house, Tirza found herself thinking, as she sipped the drink which he had passed her. She wondered why the idea of Paige and Hugo should depress her. It had nothing to do with her, after all.

Later, they dined in a dining-room rich with beams and thatch, glowing amber-shadowed mohair curtains and a table made of tamboti wood. Hugo's smile was attractive and he was using it deliberately each time he looked, or spoke, to Paige. Tirza felt numb and unreal and asked herself what she was doing in this house. At twenty-three she was in a position to choose her own accommodation, but in view of the fact that she wanted her father to take her into the business and, what was more, had the farm in the Karroo lined up as a base for a weaving industry, she had allowed herself to be placed in this impossible position.

'Well, Tirza, did you buy from the Swazi Signature?' asked Paige, and Tirza, looking at her, knew at once that her trials were only just beginning.

Aware of Hugo's eyes on her, she said, 'No, I didn't. In any case, by the time I visited there they were about to close.'

'Oh, so you came to buy?' Hugo looked at Tirza with an expression that unnerved her. 'You didn't say. What exactly did you have in mind?' Something like interest stirred in his eyes.

'That's a leading question,' she answered lightly. 'You see, I'm not quite sure. I would like to buy something before I leave Swaziland . . . from what I've seen of Cathy's curtains, carpets and upholstery.'

'And of course you'll be buying on a large scale. That follows.' Paige looked at Tirza.

It was obvious that Paige and Cathy were trying to force her into being the one to confess to Hugo Harrington that she was here not only to model for him but to buy for Harper's and, what was more important, get ideas from the Swazi Signature so that she could begin to go about starting her own weaving industry in the Karroo, which of course would create opposition—when one thought about it.

'Come on, Tirza, confess why you're here, in the first place.' Paige's eyes were glittering with mockery.

'Confess?' Tirza's voice was cool. 'I don't understand, Paige. Cathy, this is a smooth wine, isn't it?' She held her glass between her eyes and the candlelight so that the deep glow of the wine was emphasised.

'I'm glad you like it,' Cathy answered, and her thoughts could be seen in her eyes. Well, Tirza thought, she would tell Hugo, in her own time.

There were no fires on the Mudzimba range now. They had been left dampened and smouldering by the rain. The flames had, at first, been tamed and then put out, to smoulder in places.

After dinner they went through to the lounge where coffee was served and, for a while, conversation revolved around the forthcoming fashion show at the Royal Swazi Hotel. Tirza joined in the discussion and refused to let Paige see that she was affected by her remarks.

'Tell me,' Paige said, later, 'where are you taking

me tonight?' She glanced at Hugo with her sweetly composed, spiteful eyes, her blonde hair falling in tiny bleached-tipped petals, hugging her small head and clinging to her neck. For such a short girl, Tirza found herself thinking, Paige's neck was really very long and slender. Her smooth tanned face was controlled, like the rest of her, and she seldom smiled outright.

At that particular moment, however, the telephone on a small writing bureau began to ring and Cathy went to answer it, and then, after a few words, punctuated by soft laughter, she called out, 'For you, Tirza. It's your father.'

By the time Douglas Harper had finished talking to his daughter, Paige and Hugo had left for the Casino.

They had not wasted much time, Tirza thought, but at least their absence gave her time to get herself together.

After a period of desultory conversation she said, 'Cathy, are they engaged? Hugo and Paige?'

'No, not yet. I suppose *you* have somebody waiting for you, back in Cape Town, Tirza?'

'Well, nobody special.' Tirza shrugged. 'Would you mind terribly if I went to bed? I'm really tired.' She tried to smile.

'Not at all. We'll talk later, Tirza. Catch up on things—you know. I'll be interested to hear everything.' Cathy spoke on a cool note, although she was smiling.

'Yes, I'd like that. It seems strange when you consider—what might have been, Cathy.'

'You mean because at one time your father

happened to be my major preoccupation?' Cathy
laughed lightly. 'Well, yes, I nearly did marry him.
He's a fascinating and attractive man, but I came
to the conclusion that I'm happier living my own
life in my own way. I should have felt so restricted
in the Karroo. I'd hate life to become a habit.'

Later, as she prepared for bed, Tirza found herself seething. It was a pity, she thought, that Cathy
had not confessed her desire to live her life her
own way before D.H. had embarked on the alterations to the house—or at least before work on it
had progressed too far.

Turning out her bedside light, she lay staring into
the darkness. She had come a long way to make a
complete fool of herself.

Paige had already left for Mbabane by the time
she joined Cathy for breakfast the following morning. They ate on a semi-enclosed veranda which
overlooked a spectacular view of the Mudzimba
range. The mauve sprays of petria, each tiny flower
a work of art, stood out sharply against the white
pillars. Raindrops still glinted on the flowers and
the breeze was cool, although there was a real
threat of heat to come.

'Cathy,' Tirza's voice was stilted, 'I've been
thinking. I'd like to hire a car while I'm here—it
would save a lot of trouble all round. As it is,
you're kindly putting me up. How do I go about
this? There must be a place in Mbabane?'

She detected Cathy's annoyance, controlled
though it was. 'I suppose you feel you'd be able to
get around more, is that it? On your own? Don't
forget, though, I'm also involved in the fashion

show and I'll be driving out to the Royal Swazi Hotel to prepare for it. We can travel together.' Cathy spoke in the kind of voice that had the power to put her at a disadvantage, Tirza thought.

'I hadn't forgotten, Cathy, but there are certain things I'd like to do on my own—visit the market-places, and so on.'

'Well, okay, if that's what you want,' Cathy replied. 'I'll look up the telephone number for you. They'll deliver the car here, by the way. Hugo seemed surprised to hear that you had intentions of buying, didn't he? He'll be even more surprised to hear that you intend making a study of how to go about starting a weaving industry. I suppose you had in mind using his place as a kind of show-piece?' Cathy helped herself to fruit, then glanced up.

Tirza's green eyes darkened with anger. 'You put your own twist on it, Cathy. It's not really that way. It sounds awful, the way you put it.'

Ignoring the remark, Cathy said, 'Hugo's part-ner's name is Seymour. He's married and lives on the other side of town. He supervises the running of the industry in Swaziland and Hugo has this other place in Cape Town, of course, where the goods are sent. Perhaps Cape Town is big enough to cope, though, with an influx?' There was an undercurrent of meaning to her words.

'You're exaggerating, of course.' Although it was an effort to speak calmly Tirza even managed a smile.

The Mazda 323 arrived soon after lunch and Tirza lost no time in getting out of the Mobray

house, explaining to Cathy that she wanted to do a
spot of sightseeing while she was in Swaziland.

When she reached the turn-off, however, she
slackened speed and then, after a moment of indecision, she turned the car in the direction of the
Swazi Signature.

Now that there was no rain and the sun was
shining, it was easy to spot the showroom and
office complex, which was on the opposite side of
the drive leading to the studio.

In a kind of shed nearby, raw mohair hung in
the sun to dry. The yarn had been dyed and the
range of vibrant colours was exciting.

There was a charm and allure that anyone would
find hard to resist about the settlement. There was
the cheerful sound of laughter and talk, as Swazi
women, in traditional vivid coloured garments and
beehive hairstyles, went about weaving, spinning,
carding and dyeing.

The building was white and had a thatched roof.
Glass-paned French doors opened out to a paved
veranda which had no roof, but there was a low
parapet wall and there were tubs of petunias,
adding more colour to everything. In this wide-
open setting, beneath a golden yellow sun, the perfume coming from the flowers was haunting,
somehow. There was also a low table, into which a
sun-umbrella had been inserted, and white chairs,
upholstered in yellow.

Hugo was alone in the showroom and he looked
up. Looking at him, Tirza sensed, immediately,
that he had found out. 'Hello,' she was confused.
'It—it looks quite different in the sunshine, doesn't

it? The whole settlement, I mean.' She was wearing cocoa-coloured slacks and a white shirt, open low at the neckline, and Hugo looked at her for what seemed an endless moment before he said, 'Why don't you come straight out with it?' She saw that his dark blue eyes appeared almost black with anger and his mouth was hard. It was perfectly obvious that Paige and Cathy had been to work. Before she could reply he went on, 'Where shall we begin? Well, the carpets, rugs, tapestries and fabrics are sent to agents in Johannesburg, Cape Town and other main cities, not to mention smaller towns—and, by the way, remind me to make a list of all the names and addresses for you. However, the goods which you see here are also sold here, in Swaziland, to visitors and tourists. Forgive me for being sensitive about it, but I happen to be allergic to any form of underhandedness, Miss Theron.' So he still did not know her name!

Before she could even begin to defend herself he went on, 'Those long skirts and caftans over there, all in vivid and striking colours, command haute couture prices among cosmopolitan leaders of fashion. Okay?' His dark blue shirt was open to his waist and he was wearing cream levis and a wide leather belt, which seemed to emphasise his strength and masculinity.

Tirza drew in a breath, but he waved her aside. 'Now, about dyes—you remember you were eavesdropping when I happened to be discussing this on the Eastern Boulevard—they're fast colours and everything, of course, is mothproof. We use a *Swiss* chemical—I'll let you have the name of it—with the result that it's colour-fast. Before you're finished with Swaziland, I'll drive you out to my bungalow and we'll really go into this for you. I don't want you coming all this way for nothing!' His tone was cutting.

'Please,' she tried to defend herself, 'I drove out here again to tell you—to explain ... actually, I wanted to the first time.' Everything about him seemed to forbid argument and the need to explain herself to him suddenly went out of her. She felt deflated and knew the need to cry. 'I came here to explain, but you won't give me a chance. Now that I have come, I have no further obligation in the matter. I'll leave immediately for Cape Town.'

'You'll go home *after* you've fulfilled your contract with me, both in Swaziland and in the Game Reserve. I know you said that contracts are made to be broken, but in this case, Miss Theron, you will keep the contract.' He dismissed her with a careless turn of his shoulder. For a moment she stared at him in bewilderment and then, tears stinging her eyes, she turned and ran out to the Mazda.

She was amazed when he came after her and then, reaching out, he caught hold of her shoulders and swung her around to face him. His blue eyes blazed into hers. His hard, tanned fingers possessed unexpected strength. 'You will do well to remember this,' he said. His hands moved down the length of her arms and then closed about her buttocks, and she watched, with a kind of awe, while he bent his head and then his lips were upon her own. His kiss rocked her very being and any reasoning power to try to stop him.

'I hate you!' she told him, when at last he let her go.

'If you really think that, you should have stopped me,' he told her.

'I didn't have a chance,' she said, and was quick to notice one dark eyebrow lift in cynical disbelief.

With tears of anger and humiliation she drove off, and the tears dried on her cheeks in the sun and the breeze which found their way into the car. Her tears dried in the sun like the raw mohair yarn which hung out on fences.

Hugo Harrington, she thought bitterly, had mentioned that he was 'sensitive' about these things, but there was a cold confidence about him and if he had any sensitivity at all he kept it hidden under surface hardness.

Choking back tears, she drove past small banana plantations, avocado pear trees and vivid splashes of purple bougainvillaea-draped and white-walled cottages. The heat, after the rain, was intense and her shirt began to cling to her back. Her slacks felt like a ton weight against her legs.

Apparently Cathy had gone out and, thankful for small mercies, Tirza went straight to her room and began to feel a little calmer, but the knowledge that she had made herself ridiculous before all these people was never very far from her mind.

Cathy, she was told when she went out to the veranda overlooking the valley and the mountain range, would not be back until six o'clock, and Tirza felt the need to get away from the house. She found herself wishing that she could see some humour in the situation in which she had landed herself, but she could not. To keep herself occupied, she drove up to the main road and turned in the direction of Mbabane. Under different circumstances she would have felt excitement at the thought of visiting the market-place, about which she had heard so much, for Swaziland, she knew, was richly endowed with talented artists and craftsmen.

However, she was soon fascinated by the atmosphere at the market-place, which she had found without any trouble. She watched Swazi women stringing beads, admired the various white-fringed sisal table-mats, wooden hand-carved bowls, huge African masks and carvings and curtains made from porcupine quills. The idea of returning to Cathy's house filled her with such despair that she held her breath every time she thought about it. She had made up her mind on one thing, though, and that was that she intended letting Cathy know that, contrary to her father's wishes, she intended moving to one of the hotels.

It was obvious that the business rush hour was taking place in this busy and colourful town of Mbabane, the administrative capital of Swaziland, and before getting into the car, Tirza stood with wide, astonished eyes at the sight of small buses rushing at great speed and overtaking everything.

Then she got into the car and soon found herself in the stream of traffic and, unused to the Mazda, she concentrated on the heavy traffic, for although she was used to driving in traffic, the motorists in this part of the world seemed oblivious to the many warnings on the roadside and the reminders of the number of people who had lost their lives on various blind rises and sharp bends on the main road out to the Mobray house.

Cathy and Paige were not yet home and, feeling restless and unhappy, Tirza took a bath. She was still in the water when Cathy arrived and a moment later she could hear the phone ringing. When Cathy called out, 'Phone for you, Tirza—just wrap a towel around yourself and take it,' her eyes widened with concern. Who could be ringing her? she wondered.

When she entered the lounge she said, 'Is it my father?'

'No. It's Hugo.' Cathy sounded strained.

Tirza was unable to keep the surprise from her voice. 'Hugo?'

'That's what I said.' Cathy went on staring at her, as though this was a situation that demanded careful analysis.

Standing in Cathy's elegant lounge, with a large towel draped about her and her toes, which she had dried hurriedly, digging into the mohair carpet, she got herself under control with effort. 'Yes?'

From where she was standing she could see the Mudzimba mountain range and the smoke that curled upwards from mountain fires which had started smouldering again.

'I usually go out of my way to entertain business associates,' Hugo was saying, 'and, since you're one, I'm taking you to dinner.'

After a moment she said, 'I wouldn't want you to go out of your way for me, so I decline your invitation. In any case, it seems strange. Why should you want to have dinner with me?' She put her knuckles against her teeth.

'Not just with you,' he said, 'I wouldn't want to be so involved.' He spoke with unveiled sarcasm. 'I want you to meet the other girls who'll be modelling with you.'

'Surely that's not necessary?' She kept her voice carefully expressionless.

'I'll pick you up at eight,' he went on with complete indifference. 'We'll be going to the Royal Swazi Spa—so dress up.'

'Do the others know?' she asked, keeping her voice very soft.

'The others?' Her fingers tightened at the terseness in his voice.

'You know perfectly well who I mean,' she said, still in that soft expressionless voice. 'Do I have to inform them?'

'You're missing the point. The others, as you call them, will not be going, since they already know these girls.'

Immediately Tirza replaced the receiver she went back to her room where she stood gazing out of the windows. Did Paige and Cathy know about this arrangement? Dragging her fingers through her damp hair, she felt almost suffocated by everything and longed for a suitable opportunity to present itself whereby she could thank Cathy for her hospitality and tell her, at the same time, that she would be leaving.

Cathy was in the lounge, with Paige, when she went through, still wearing her dressing-gown. Tall glasses stood defrosting on a small table.

'Did you know that Hugo Harrington has arranged for me to have dinner at the Royal Swazi Spa—along with his other models?' she asked. The frosty silence in the room was an indication that the two women did know. 'I'm sorry,' she went on, seething inside, 'if I'd only known about it I'd have let you know that I wouldn't be here for dinner, Cathy.' In a detached way she found herself wondering whether she should allow the rage she was feeling to get the better of her and let these two have a piece of her mind and then, in a diminished voice, she said, 'Why did you tell Hugo Harrington about my intention to start a weaving industry? What's more, why did you purposely create a completely wrong impression? It's made me out to be some kind of spy, to meet my own ends. I didn't come here to spy, just put that on record, will you? I came here to buy. I'll admit that I was interested to see the Swazi Signature industry . . .'

'You are, nevertheless, here under false pretences,' Paige sounded vicious. 'You came here to snoop—it's as simple as that.'

'I did not! I came here to model. Primarily, Paige, I came here to model for him. Secondly, I intended buying for Harper's. There's nothing against buying from a weaving industry, is there? *Any* weaving industry. Harper's buy from an industry in Lesotho.'

'For some unknown reason you appear to be interested in the Swaziland weavers. At a guess, I would say you were going to use your purchases as samples.' Paige's small face was like a spiteful mask.

'You have a nerve, to suggest such a rotten thing! How can you be sure that's what I was going to do? The purchases were going to various Harper complexes and I was going to tell him so.'

'You yourself told my mother that you intended to *scout around*, to use your very own words, because you intend starting your own weaving industry. In other words,' Paige continued with malice, 'you're here to find out how to go about it—and at Hugo's expense, right?'

Tirza felt hopeless and knew that whatever she had to say would count for nothing.

'I find all this very unsettling,' Cathy cut in, 'and that's putting it mildly.'

'I can understand that,' said Tirza, on a hard breath, 'and for this reason, Cathy, I'm going to leave here. I'll go to one of the Holiday Inns.'

'Why don't you just leave Swaziland?' Paige asked. 'After all, you don't have to model.'

'Although it really has nothing to do with you,' Tirza said, 'I suggested breaking my contract, but Hugo Harrington refused. I can't think why, except perhaps that he sees fit to humiliate me further. Actually, my father was being perfectly ridiculous in involving you with my visit here.'

They made no attempt to stop her when she left the room, and once she had packed, she left. There seemed to be no point in saying goodbye. It was humiliating, but even more humiliating was the fact that she had appeared humiliated in front of Cathy and Paige Mobray.

Hugo Harrington, she thought, could find out

for himself that she had left the Mobray house.
Now perhaps she could think again—could cry.

Because she did not quite know what to do, she
drove straight to the Royal Swazi Hotel and
booked in as Miss Tirza Theron.

The hotel and spa had not yet begun its night
life and she had had no trouble in finding space on
one of the parking terraces. She had been aware of
the traffic swishing by on the National Road at the
bottom of the hotel gardens as she had made her
way into the hotel, and a wildness within her which
was almost too unbearable to stand.

Her room and private bathroom were everything
she could wish for, and she sank down on the
kingsize bed, with its exciting Spanish-type bedhead and thickly embossed burnt-orange, gold and
pale yellow bedcover. Hugo Harrington, she
thought, would just have to make the discovery
that she had left Cathy's house when he called for
her later on in the evening.

He phoned at eight-thirty. Getting straight to the
point, he said, 'I gathered you might have gone to
the Royal Swazi Spa.'

'I couldn't let you know.'

'My number is in the book.' He sounded hostile.
'I'm in the foyer, waiting.'

'You can wait. I'm not a mouse for you to play
with, merely because I was fool enough to sign on
the dotted line. Besides, I'm not dressed for
dining.'

'Well, *get* dressed.' She gasped when, at his end,
he put the phone down on her and she stood staring at the receiver in her hand for a moment.

Then she went to one of her cases and took out a voluminous, billowing, brilliant coloured bolero and skirt extravaganza in shocking-pink, apple-green and black, which left her midriff bare. When she was dressed she expertly applied eye-shadow and mascara, coloured her lips and added a touch of lip-gloss. Leaving the ornate lamps burning, she made her way to the heavy Spanish-type door and then hesitated.

'Why *should* I go?' she whispered fiercely. 'I'll phone D.H. and tell him what a mess I'm in ... it's as simple as that.'

Hugo Harrington chose that moment to knock on the door and when she opened it he stepped right into the small corridor. He was wearing a dinner suit with a frilled white shirt and black tie which could not disguise the graceful animal-like magnetism about him, or the dangerous quality she had noticed about him at the weaving settlement.

'I made an appointment with you—and the other girls for ...' he glanced at his watch, 'approximately one hour ago. Anyway,' his voice was scathing, 'that was roughly the idea.' His dark blue eyes went over her. 'However, I'm glad to see you're ready at last and looking quite ravishing into the bargain. Let's go.' He put his fingers on her wrist and she could feel the proprietorial grip which was so definitely male.

'You're hurting me!' She glanced down at his fingers and felt her anger rising.

'I *mean* to hurt you.' His eyes did not leave her face.

'What are you getting out of this?' she asked.

'What difference can it possibly make to you whether I model or not?'

'You signed a contract and you will not break it. I'm just not used to this sort of treatment, Miss Theron.' His voice chilled her.

'And you mean to play your part in convincing me, is that it?' She shook her wrist free and stood rubbing it, her breath coming fast. 'And while we're about it, just you keep your hands off me! When I signed that contract, mauling me didn't enter into it. Besides, signing a contract means nothing.'

'There are certain principles to abide by, Miss Theron.'

'What, for instance?'

'Well, that persuasion is better than force, for instance. Are you coming? I don't want to have to force you.'

Feeling trapped by his close proximity, Tirza made to open the heavy door, but he brushed her aside and did this himself.

Hugo led the way to the cocktail bar and Tirza walked beside him with a natural grace, her tawny hair bouncing about her shoulders.

To reach the cocktail bar they had to go down several shallow steps and, catching her heel in her long gown, she stumbled. Without thinking, she took his arm and directly she had recovered her balance she snatched her hand away.

To her surprise, the girls who were going to model for Hugo were escorted by young men, and Tirza felt a surge of relief. Being in a mixed party would simplify matters, give her time to compose herself.

Beside her, in the dimly-lit space, Hugo held his glass with his fingertips around the rim. Tirza appeared poised, chic and remarkably self-possessed, but her mind was a network of anxieties. Her nerves screamed with impatience for this night to be over, and she wondered what time they were supposed to dine and imagined the huge round table which would accommodate them all.

She was amazed, therefore, when they were in the foyer of the hotel to hear Hugo say, 'Well, until rehearsals tomorrow . . . goodnight.'

When they were alone she said, 'I'm afraid I don't understand. I thought we were all going to have dinner together? That's what you said.'

His eyes brushed over her. 'That's not what I said. What I *did* say, and I quote, was that I usually go out of my way to entertain business associates and, since you are one, I'm taking you to dinner.'

Feeling furious with him, she retorted, 'I remember, word for word, what you said. You said, and *I quote*—not just with you. I wouldn't want to be so involved.'

'You're gifted, it would appear, with a most remarkable memory. Well, I have a reputation for changing my mind.'

'For that matter, so do I have a reputation for changing my mind—and I've now changed my mind about having dinner!' She turned her furious green gaze on him.

Hugo took her arm. 'Look, we're going to see a lot of each other over the next couple of weeks and I have a number of things I want to discuss with you.'

Moving away from him she said, 'I can't think what there is to discuss.'

'You're going to work for me—isn't that enough to go on?'

'It would appear that apart from creating a whole lot of unpleasant hassles for myself, I have no option but to work for you. I can't imagine what you have to discuss with me privately. What about those other girls?'

'Those girls often model for Swazi Signature. They're aware of the ropes. Now stop arguing.' He took her arm and led the way to the dining-room.

Soon after they had been shown to their table they were given the menu, which they studied before ordering. Tirza felt a thrill at being with Hugo Harrington. Automatically, her eyes went to him, just as he turned to look at her and in the dim light, their eyes met and held. The look was like a two-way magnet. She felt it and she knew he felt it.

'My head dyer is right,' he said, very softly, 'you are very beautiful. The man you call Nigel knew what he was about.'

Looking at him, across the small round table, her eyes glowed malevolently. 'The way you speak only serves to show up your true character.'

'Really? Could you be more explicit?' His eyes lingered, with lazy insolence, on her mouth.

'You're cold and calculating. Why bring him up?'

'You know where you stand with me—in this case. I do have a cold and calculating character. In other words, I expect things between you and the

Mobrays to run smoothly during the next couple of weeks. Okay?'

'And you brought me here just to tell me *that*?'

'Yes.'

While they were waiting for a very special dessert, which had to be especially prepared for them, Hugo asked her to dance.

'I think you misunderstand the situation,' she said. 'This happens to be a business appointment. There's absolutely no need for me to dance with you.'

'Let's not fool ourselves,' he replied, 'the music is good and we would both like to dance to it.'

'It isn't compulsory to dance.' She realised that she was being childish, but went on, 'It says nothing about dancing in the contract, because I've studied it.'

'To everything there's a social side. As a buyer, you should know that.'

Tirza gestured helplessly, trying to convey the futility of arguing with him.

They walked on to the dance floor, and men at various tables looked up from their food to look at her, while others momentarily broke off what they were saying. Before taking her into his arms, Hugo studied her for a moment, as though deciding to reappraise her.

The music, at this stage, was slow, with a slow beat, and necessitated close contact, and while they were dancing, from beneath her lashes Tirza discovered that the angles of Hugo Harrington's cheekbones and jaw were sculptured and she felt her nerves begin to tighten up. It was not the first time she realised that she was more than just a little attracted to him.

Finally they went back to their table and the Don Pedro dessert was served.

'Where is the casino?' Tirza asked. 'It seems so quiet. One would expect more activity in a hotel with a gambling casino.'

'We'll drop in later.' He gave her a brief smile.

'Thank you.'

The casino was dimly lit and filled with smoke and click-clack noises, and the intensity of the people around the tables struck Tirza with considerable force. The clientele was mostly what she supposed could be described as 'jet-set'. The expressions of the croupiers, at their tables, seemed bored and blank.

She found herself whispering, 'This kind of sophistication is almost frightening, isn't it?' The heavy gold earrings she was wearing glinted. When Hugo took her arm, she allowed him to get away with it. 'Come and stand over here,' he said, and she experienced an odd little thrill.

The roulettes continued to spin and the air was electric with fortunes being lost by the minute. Tirza's eyes began to burn and she touched her cheeks with her fingertips.

'Is the smoke worrying you?' Hugo asked, his eyes on her face.

Laughing a little, she said, 'Yes. I'm not used to it—it's so thick.'

'I don't think the smell of it could ever be eradicated from this place,' he said. He had his charming side, obviously, and was demonstrating it now, she thought.

At that moment she caught a glimpse of Cathy and Paige at one of the tables on the other side of the casino. Both women were gambling and both were wearing the same calculating expression. It was obvious that they had come here to gamble and knew what they were about. Could this be one of the reasons why Cathy had not gone through with the marriage to her father?

There was a mixture of races, but on each face there was the same calculating expression. They had all come here for one thing, and that was to gamble, and to gamble heavily. Many of the older women were beautifully gowned and bejwelled, while the young women wore no jewels and very little make-up.

Beside her, Hugo said, 'Would you like to try?'

'I wouldn't know where to begin. No—thank you.' After a moment she asked, 'What about you?'

'Gambling isn't something I take very seriously,' he told her.

For a while she watched him, and although she knew nothing about what was taking place at the table she had the feeling that he was winning. At the far end, she could see Cathy and Paige preparing to leave, and it was obvious that Hugo had not noticed them.

Afterwards she said, laughing a little, 'You've won some money?'

'You brought me luck,' he replied. 'Come along, let's go and collect it.'

When they had done this they went out to the foyer from where they could see the garden, which was festooned with coloured lights and, without thinking, Tirza said, 'I'd love to get some fresh air, after all that smoke. It was so stuffy in the casino.'

'That's not a bad idea,' he agreed.

When he reached for her in the garden she found it impossible to resist him and found herself becoming excited and strained against him. Against her mouth he said, 'I couldn't let you come all this way for nothing, could I? What do I get in return?' He held her away from him and looked down at her.

'Don't you ever say that to me again! I don't want anything from you.' Humiliation washed over her.

'You came to Swaziland to use me,' he shrugged. 'What's to stop me from using you?'

Numbly, she stared at him, feeling his words like a whiplash. 'Are you trying to tell me that because I signed a contract this gives you the prerogative to force your attentions on me?'

'Force?' He laughed softly.

Turning away from him, Tirza ran through the garden in the direction of the main entrance to the hotel and, once inside, she went straight to her room with its ornate lamps and sliding glass wall, giving access to the balcony. She was too angry to cry and sank down on the kingsize bed and stared at nothing. After a while she sat up, then lifted the phone and dialled her father's number in Cape Town. She would have to speak to him about the ridiculous contract. There must be a way out of it, without having the Harper name dragged into court, she thought. She had also committed the offence of not signing her true name. At the other end of the line the phone kept on ringing and ringing until, finally, she put the receiver back on its cradle. Her father was out—as usual. 'You seem to forget I'm your daughter,' she muttered aloud. 'You seem to forget that I might just need you now and then.'

Her room seemed very quiet, but then she was used to this. Her father's Cape-style mansion always seemed extra quiet when he was away on a business trip. The feeling that she had now, though, this wild, restless feeling, was different. It was a feeling which had Hugo Harrington at its starting point. Her eyes were wide and green and confused. One moment she had thought that she couldn't survive without Nigel Wright and the next moment she had known that she could. And what was more confusing was the fact that she realised, now, that she could pinpoint the exact moment . . . and that was when she had turned, in her stool at the Holiday Inn, on the Eastern Boulevard, to speak to Hugo Harrington.

CHAPTER FIVE

In the morning, Tirza ate breakfast at the poolside. After lunch there was to be a rehearsal of the fashion show and so, until then, she was free to mope, for that was all it amounted to. So far, it appeared, to Hugo Harrington she was still Tirza Theron, since apparently Cathy and Paige, unaware of the fact that Hugo knew her by this name, had not put him wise.

She was wearing white slacks and a floral shirt, the collar of which framed her face. Her hair was drawn back in a smooth elegant style and she had an air of confidence about her. She was extremely chic and there was nothing to show that she was being torn by conflicting feelings.

After a while she stripped down to her bikini and dived into the glittering blue water. Later she sunbathed and, all the time, her mind was busy with the problems she had so unwittingly created for herself. Even the buying for Harper's had come to nothing, she thought a little wildly. Everything she had intended had collapsed about her. In short, she had succeeded in making a fool of herself. Her mood improved a little after the swim and the warmth of the sun and she even found herself thinking that she would buy where and when she deemed fit. This entire hideous episode would be in the interest of Harper's, and the fact that she had to carry out the contract to model for Swazi Signature would take second place, so far as she was concerned.

Skipping lunch, she went to her room and took a shower, then changed into fresh slacks and a shirt to go with them and went along to the reception room which had been allotted to the Swazi Signature for the purpose of putting on a series of fashion shows.

The girls she had met the night before were already there, but there was no sign of Cathy and Paige. When they did arrive it was with Hugo. There was no sign of recognition in his eyes as he glanced carelessly in Tirza's direction.

'Okay,' his dark blue eyes flickered from beautiful face to beautiful face, 'let's get down to business.' He was wearing white trousers and a dark-green shirt and he looked fabulous, Tirza found herself thinking. Part of his sex appeal was the mystery which seemed so much a part of him. The kind of mystery which made you wonder how deeply he felt. Just how deeply *could* he feel?

The two Mobray women barely glanced at her, which really made no difference as they were all soon caught up in the changing world of fashion. Creations in mohair conjured up the distant lands of Morocco, Persia, India, Hungary and Turkey, not to mention Africa, and Tirza thrilled to the exotic colours and fine textures. While she changed and rechanged into the glamorous collection of clothes she was able to forget about Cathy and Paige. To go with much of the collection was an exciting assortment of jewellery made up of semiprecious stones—quartz, agate, tourmaline, rock crystal . . .

The models were efficient and were clued up to the tricks of the trade, and it was obvious that the forthcoming fashion shows were going to be profitable.

These came and went far more swiftly than Tirza imagine they would do, and without the ill-feeling she had anticipated. Both Cathy and Paige had been coldly polite and there was little to show, outwardly, that there had been ill-feeling.

Unless he had to, Hugo did not speak to her, and Tirza found herself brooding about this state of events. Ironically, her father's business had always created an impassable barrier between them, and now it was Hugo's.

Finally it was time to leave the Ezulwini Valley and Swaziland where, in the famous casino, fortunes were made, and lost, by the flick of a wrist. Even Cathy and Paige had played at one of the gaming tables with the kind of apparent skill that had made them oblivious to the fact that they were being observed.

The fashion shows had been well patronised and ended with a cheese and wine party, on a note of success. Slim and beautiful in green silk, Tirza was sipping a drink when Hugo joined her and she was more than just a little surprised when he said, 'You were very good.' Although his voice was completely impersonal her awareness of him was far from vague.

'Thank you,' she answered, lowering her lashes to look at her glass.

'As you know,' he went on, 'we leave in the morning.'

'Yes. I've already phoned the car hire people to come and collect my car,' she said.

'You were going to travel with the Mobrays in the Kombi and I was to follow in my car, about an hour later. I have an important business appointment here, first.'

'You say—*were going to travel* with the Mobrays,' she lifted her lashes and looked directly at him. 'Does this mean you're releasing me from the contract?'

'No,' his voice was abrupt. 'It doesn't mean that. It simply means that in view of the fact that you're not on good terms with them you'll be travelling with me.' There was a slight flicker in his eyes. 'I don't think they like you very much.'

The reaction was immediate. 'The dislike is mutual,' Tirza replied tartly, beginning to play with her glass. 'I've got a good mind not to go at all. I'll probably fly back home.'

'I don't advise you to try.' Hugo's eyes were suddenly ice-blue.

It was absurd to feel as excited as this, she found herself thinking.

'What time shall I be ready and waiting?' she asked, with sarcasm.

'I'm leaving about ten,' he told her, and pride kept her silent.

Moodily she watched him as he made his un-hurried way to Paige, who was standing with a cluster of people.

Turning, she gave her attention to Hugo's partners, Simon Reynolds, who had been standing next to her but had discreetly moved away when Hugo had addressed her.

She was waiting in the foyer the following morning when Hugo arrived to pick her up.

'I'm surprised Paige Mobray allowed this arrangement,' she could not help saying.

'Tch! Tch! Jealous?' he replied. 'Is this all the luggage you have?'

'Yes.' It disturbed her not to know what he felt about Paige, and then, without warning, he glanced at her with that veiled ironic smile.

When they were in the car he said, 'I can now begin to get down to a spot of relaxing. It's been quite a show.'

What was surprising was that, while he drove in the direction of Mbabane, Tirza found herself relaxing with him. Her eyes strayed in the direction of the stone-hewn mountains, where those distant fires always seemed to be burning, wattles and waving bougainvillaea, mostly of the purple and mauve variety.

Loud and colourful, the town of Mbabane was more vibrant than she remembered it. The sound of music seemed to blast the pavements and the traffic was urgent and hasty.

Hugo did not seem inclined towards conversation and Tirza knew if she tried to make small talk she would lay herself open to more of his cutting remarks, so she, too, remained silent. However, she could tell without looking at him when he was looking at her.

Once they were through the border post she

realised, with an absurd little thrill, that they were on the way. It could have been so exciting in different circumstances, she found herself thinking.

The sun was high and she longed for something to drink and was thankful when Hugo stopped at a kiosk on the roadside, where he bought fresh orange juice, which they drank there and then, sitting in the car, with the doors open to catch the breeze.

Later, they stopped for lunch and then headed for the entrance to the Game Park, where they were given the usual maps of the reserve and paper packets, with animals on them, into which all rubbish, in the form of fruit skins, sweet wrappers and so on, had to be discarded, for getting out of a vehicle was forbidden once they were in the reserve.

Suddenly Tirza felt herself beginning to tense up again. Why hadn't Hugo torn the contract in two? Why was he subjecting her to the humiliation of carrying on with this trip—especially in the company of Cathy and Paige?

They reached the camp of Satara, which looked almost deserted, but this was only because the people accommodating the bungalows in the enclosed gardens were still out spotting game, for the gates did not close until sundown.

Hugo had reserved three bungalows—one for Cathy and Paige, one for Miss Tirza Theron and one for himself. Turning to her, after he had parked the car in the space next to one of the bungalows, he said, 'You aren't going to be nervous, are you, in a bungalow by yourself?' Before she could reply he went on, 'If you are—well, we can always share one together.'

Stung by his remark, the devil in her almost prompted her to say, 'I'll put that on record, Mr Harrington, because I might just be *very* nervous!'

She was quick to notice the Swazi Signature Kombi which was parked beneath the trees, next to one of the bungalows, which meant that the other two had arrived.

With mounting frustration she watched Hugo unload their cases. 'I can manage my own, thank you,' she told him. 'One in each hand. It's no problem.' She lifted them and then turned to him again. 'Which bungalow shall I take? It's obvious that Cathy and Paige are in the first one. The Kombi has been parked next to it, as you can see.'

'Take the middle one,' he told her carelessly.

At that moment, Paige pushed open the screened-door to the small veranda of their bungalow. 'Hi,' she said, completely ignoring Tirza. 'So you've arrived? We're expecting you for sundowners, after you've got organised.'

'Consider it a date,' Hugo called.

After the heat outside, the bungalow was cool, and Tirza flopped down on one of the beds and closed her eyes. Behind her eyelids the bush still seemed to be moving and pictures of animals, as they had seen them on the drive to the camp, flitted about. After a while she opened her eyes and got up and washed her face at the wash-hand basin.

It was an attractive rest-hut, she thought, looking around. There was a shower cubicle and a screened veranda, with a small refrigerator and a table and chairs and a metal cabinet for groceries, should visitors prefer to cater for themselves rather than eat at the restaurant nearby.

Tomorrow, Tirza thought tensely, she and Paige would be modelling some of the glamorous caftans in the restaurant.

Examining herself in the mirror, she made a face. 'Why is it you appear to be attracted to unusual and unscrupulous men?' she said.

A vision of Paige came to her mind . . . proud, vain, ambitious—for anyone could see that Paige was madly ambitious. Working with her at the Royal Swazi Hotel, it had been obvious that this girl, daughter of the woman her father had nearly married, was obsessed if her hair was not just right, or if she thought she'd put on weight overnight. This preoccupation with her looks seemed to lead to nervous fatigue, and by the time they had finished modelling Paige had often been in a foul mood, snapping at Cathy or anybody who happened to be near her.

The sundowner invitation had not appeared to include her and, to show her independence, she decided to walk to the shop.

While she was in the building which was part-supermarket and part-curio shop and where she noticed there were attractive wall-hangings and mohair rugs, bearing the Swazi Signature Weaving Industry trade name, she got to listening to what people were talking about. The big topic appeared to be a waterhole, not far from the camp, where game could easily be spotted drinking just before sunset. 'We even take our sundowners there,' one woman giggled.

The words served to remind Tirza of Paige's snub and, on the spur of the moment, she bought a can of beer, although she never drank beer. She would drink her own sundowner in her own bungalow, she thought. It was as simple as that.

The conversation went on around her and it was easy to determine where this waterhole was . . . just past the gates, turn right and right again . . .

Well, parking near a waterhole at sunset should be fun, Tirza thought, feeling suddenly very depressed, *and* in the right company. Obviously she was the odd one out here.

Moodily she walked back to the bungalow and, soon after her arrival there, Hugo knocked on her screened door and she turned as he opened it and stepped up on to the veranda. 'Where have you been?' he asked. 'We were expecting you.'

'You were?' She immediately found herself on the defensive and her eyes fenced with his. 'I wasn't aware that I'd been invited. Don't patronise me!'

'Why didn't you tell me that your real name is Harper?' Looking at him, Tirza sensed the tightly-leashed anger beneath the surface of his control.

After a sickening pause she said, 'Oh, so you've finally been told? Well, that had to come, I suppose. My real name is Tirza Theron Harper, so it wasn't exactly a lie.'

'I'm sorry, I don't see the connection. So far as these matters go, your name is Tirza Harper. Right?'

'You mean so far as contracts are concerned, of course!'

'Yes, but that's only one side of the story.'

Hugo's blue eyes showed frank contempt.

'Oh, is it *so* important?' She shrugged and turned away from him.

'Yes.' She was aware, as he spoke, that he had closed the distance between them. 'It's important to me, anyway. I don't like to be taken in, either by people or situations.'

She swung round and nearly collided with him. 'You'll realise, now, perhaps, that the contract I signed doesn't happen to be valid, in view of the fact that I signed Tirza Theron.'

He cut harshly across the sentence. 'Your name happens to be Tirza Theron Harper, right? So far as I'm concerned, the contract is valid, and you will abide by it, but perhaps you'd like me to take this matter further, to prove it? Your daddy,' he drew the word out sarcastically, 'happens to be Douglas Harper. Why weren't you honest with me? Now I can see why your face looked familiar to me. It's been pictured over and over again in countless magazines. And so here you are, *Miss Harper*,' he folded his arms, 'sleek with success in the capacity of buyer and chief scout for Harper's. You're more calculating than I thought. I need a drink,' he added, on an angry breath.

With wide, troubled eyes Tirza watched him as he opened the door and then allowed it to slam behind him, as he went down the steps.

'You don't even give me a chance to explain,' she called out.

'You don't have to explain,' he called back. 'It's all been spelt out very clearly. There can be no greater boredom than that brought about by a pack of lies. I don't want to hear any more. You're a cheat, Miss Harper, and I just don't happen to like cheats.' He chilled her with his sarcasm, as he stood there at the foot of the steps looking up at her, as she held the door open.

Suddenly everything was unbearable to her. Here she was, without transport of her own, in the company of people who made no effort to conceal the fact that she was disliked. She felt bruised and bewildered and a little sick. Everything that she had told Cathy had been pounced upon and blown up out of all proportion. She knew a yearning to get away somewhere, by herself . . . the waterhole, for instance, where she could sit very quietly in a car and gaze at a pink sunset and animals venturing out to drink. From her window she caught sight of Hugo strolling in the direction of the curio shop. He was the type of man, she knew, who would become impatient with any kind of malicious gossip, even if there did happen to be truth at the back of it and it seemed obvious that he, too, wanted to be alone.

Once again she was experiencing the loneliness of being Douglas Harper's daughter.

She glanced round for her bag and the scarf which she had tied about her hair in Hugo's car, on the journey here. Apparently she had lost the scarf, and this was another prick to her tense nerves. She slipped the can of beer into the bag and decided that she would walk down to the security fence, find a comfortable place to sit and drink it. Maybe she would see animals on the other side of the fence. At this moment she would have liked nothing better than to go along to Cathy's bungalow and give vent to the anger which was building up every second. However, in order to carry out the contract which she had signed, she knew that she would have to exercise self-control.

Cathy and Paige were sitting on the small screened veranda of their bungalow, and Tirza could hear them arguing.

Hugo's Alfa-Romeo was coated with a fine layer of dust and the windows were rolled down. When she noticed her headscarf on the seat she opened the door on the passenger side and, in a fit of temper, retrieved the scarf. Hugo had left the keys in the car and her green eyes swung instantly in their direction. She looked at them solemnly for a moment, and then, acting recklessly, she slipped into the car and started the engine.

With little thought of the consequences she drove to the waterhole, and by the time she reached it, it was like arriving at a drive-in cinema. Cars were squeezed into the small sandy area and she was lucky to find a space to park.

The sun was already preparing to set and several small animals were leaving the safety of the bush to drink at the waterhole and turned to test the breeze before crossing the bare, game-trodden area between camouflage and water.

Suddenly the enormity of what she had done hit her. 'God, what have I done?' she whispered and put her knuckles against her teeth. 'Taking his car, just like that!'

She stared at the little drama at the waterhole, but her thoughts were busy on how she would get

out of this new situation. What would she say?
There was no excuse for taking Hugo's car.
Suddenly a jackal, scattering a buck and some
birds, attracted her attention and held it, and by
the time that she had made up her mind to leave
the waterhole and drive back to camp, it was too
late, for she was completely hemmed in by
vehicles.

How she would adore a long, leisurely shower,
she thought, and something to drink to calm her
screaming nerves. And then, remembering, she
reached for her bag and took out the can of beer.
Beer was better than nothing, she mused.

The sky was beginning to flame and it enhanced
that spell which was simply known as 'the bush'.
Strangely enough, the beer had a calming effect
and she felt almost at peace, ready to face anything.

Idly her eyes scanned the faces of the occupants
in those cars which were parked on a rise, in a
half-moon, round the waterhole. When she saw
Hugo watching her from the Swazi Signature
Kombi her green eyes widened and then registered
shock. She saw the anger on his face. In the next
car a child was shouting, 'Look, Mummy, a whole
herd of elephants!'

Tirza's shocked eyes swung away and she caught
her breath at the sight of the herd which had
ambled out of the dry bush. The great beasts
moved towards the water. Except for the calves,
they were so huge, and yet quite soundless. It was
an eerie, breathtaking experience and Tirza was
caught up in it. Regardless of Hugo Harrington,
who was sitting in the Kombi, and the anger in

him which was wrestling to be released, she reached
for her bag and took out her Nikon camera and
then opening the door she slipped her legs out of
the car and stood up, camera held in position. It
made no difference to her, at the moment, that she
was in for a showdown with Hugo Harrington in
the near future.

He was beside her, it seemed, in an instant and
in one lithe movement. 'What the devil do you
think you're doing? Get back into the car!'

When she was back in the car and he was next
to her he said angrily, 'Visitors to the reserve are
requested not to leave the safety of their vehicles.'
With wide eyes she watched him as he shrugged
off the jacket he was wearing and tossed it on to
the back seat. 'You'd do well to remember that, in
future.' She was aware of those dark blue eyes and
was shocked at the anger in them, behind their
thick black growth of lashes. His expression chilled
her and she had had nothing to say for herself.

In the car next to them a man was complaining
in a loud voice. 'What the devil do those two think
they're up to? If those animals charged, we
wouldn't have a snowball's chance in hell. We're
completely blocked in here by cars ... can't even
reverse and turn, until some of them get away
first.'

'We are parked next to a very precise man,'
Hugo went on, still in that angry voice, 'and I
heartily endorse what he has to say.'

'I ... I'm ...' Tirza started to say, but he inter-
rupted her rudely. 'Save it, Miss Harper. It's a
wonder you hadn't arranged for a representative

of the *News of the World* to be present!'

Humiliation washing over her she turned miserably away from him. The elephants were beginning to drink now. The great bulk of an elephant produced a shock and exercised fear, mingled with fascination. The bull elephants were much larger than the females and had powerful tusks and broad-based trunks. The tusks of the cows were slender and three nurslings pressed themselves against their mothers who, encouraging them to drink, shoved them on with their trunks. It was so silent, Tirza found herself thinking. The animals had moved out of the bush as silently as a lizard. They sucked up the water with their trunks and then poured it into their mouths. A very small calf did not drink, but its mother sprayed it all over and it began to squeal immediately, and made to run away, but was held back. The squealing of the calf instantly caused a rustle of panic on the part of the game-spotters.

In the car next to them the man was talking again, still in that same loud voice. 'I don't like this,' he was saying. 'I don't like this at all. I reckon we try to get away from here before they charge. If they do, mark my words, panic is going to set in. There'll be a pile-up equal to none, quite apart from the fact that those animals could make concertinas of the cars.'

Tirza was feeling tight with tension, and added to this was the fact that she had blatantly helped herself to Hugo's car and was going to have to answer for it.

The protective movements of the female elephants towards their young increased the feeling of anticipation. The cows seemed almost to be nursing calves between their thick legs and they began brushing the calves' heads with their trunks.

A giant elephant stood slightly apart from the rest, showering his head and great body. He had been the last to arrive, and as he stopped and fanned his huge ears, there was more agitation on the part of the game-spotters.

Immediately the first car started, all the others followed. Panic was beginning to take over and people who honoured the trusting and unwritten code that doors to rest-huts were left unlocked were showing the ugly side to their natures as they swore at other people who might be blocking the way to escape and, in so doing, jeopardised the endeavour to save the skins of their families and themselves.

Hugo, who was now in the driver's seat, made no attempt to start the Alfa-Romeo, and Tirza realised that if panic had its way somebody was going to have to give, for there were children, and even babies, in some of the cars.

The whole peaceful sunset scene was changing into a kind of nightmare of anticipation.

At the waterhole, one of the calves huddled against its mother, searching for the source of the sound of engines, and this movement was immediately followed by the loud trumpeting of the giant elephant.

There was a fresh surge of panic and then, in the midst of all this panic and confusion, the herd wheeled and, in their strange, shambling, and almost comical run, made for the bush on the

What made Marge burn the toast and miss her favorite soap opera?

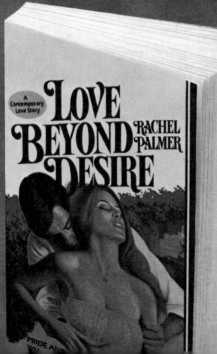

A Contemporary Love Story

LOVE BEYOND DESIRE

RACHEL PALMER

...At his touch, her body felt a familiar wild stirring, but she struggled to resist it. This is not love, she thought bitterly.

PRIDE AND

*A compelling love story of
mystery and intrigue…
conflicts and jealousies…
and a forbidden love that
threatens to shatter the lives
of all involved with the
aristocratic Lopez family.*

← Mail this card today for your FREE gifts.

TAKE THIS BOOK
AND TOTE BAG FREE!

Mail to: **SUPER OMANCE**
1440 South Priest Drive, Tempe, Arizona 85281

YES, please send me FREE and without any obligation, my
SUPER OMANCE novel, *Love Beyond Desire*. If you do not hear
from me after I have examined my FREE book, please send me
the 4 new **SUPER OMANCE** books every month as soon as they
come off the press. I understand that I will be billed only $2.50 per
book (total $10.00). There are no shipping and handling or any
other hidden charges. There is no minimum number of books that
I have to purchase. In fact, I may cancel this arrangement at any
time. *Love Beyond Desire* and the tote bag are mine to keep as
FREE gifts even if I do not buy any additional books.

134-CIS-KADE

Name	(Please Print)
Address	Apt. No.
City	
State	Zip
Signature	(If under 18, parent or guardian must sign.)

This offer is limited to one order per household and not valid to present subscribers.
We reserve the right to exercise discretion in granting membership. If price changes
are necessary you will be notified. Offer expires July 31, 1983.

PRINTED IN U.S.A.   **SUPER OMANCE**

opposite side of the water. Silent, and without charging, that was the miracle of it all ... Tirza allowed herself to sag and a long-pent-up breath escaped her. She and Hugo were the only two people who were not trying to make a getaway. Eventually, they were the only people left in the raised clearing which looked down on the waterhole, with its almost creamy coffee-coloured water.

He made no attempt to say anything and she was determined not to be the first to speak. A tall, awkward bird with prancing steps approached the waterhole and, to calm her shrieking nerves, Tirza kept her eyes on it.

And then Hugo spoke. 'What the hell are you up to?'

She turned her head to look at him and saw his eyes on the beer can which she had placed on the open flap of the glove compartment, and her heartbeats threatened to suffocate her.

'In Swaziland,' he went on, 'you arrived in a storm and you boasted about your enjoyment of ... nature's pyrotechnics. Now I find you here, complete with sundowner and this fine network of nerves of yours completely unruffled to the fact that you were in danger the minute you stepped out of the car with your Nikon. Not only that, you endangered the lives of those about you.' Listening to him, she was ashamed to admit, even to herself, that his every movement held an overwhelming fascination for her and, without replying, she brushed back a wisp of hair from her cheek.

'What did you expect me to do,' he continued,

'when I saw you pass through the gates in my car
. . . run up a flag?'

'Yes,' she said, on a small furious breath, 'that's
exactly what I did expect.'

'That's the sort of answer I should have
expected. You have a passion for the dramatic and,
very often, the absurd.'

When she made no reply he said, 'Are you
listening to me?'

'Oh . . .' she shrugged in what she hoped was a
careless fashion, 'intently.' To stop herself from
shaking she hugged herself and then after a
moment she said, 'I'm sorry about the car. I—I
don't know what got into me.'

The flaming colours in the sky were fading and
the air was cooler.

'Anyway, we'll save it,' Hugo was saying, 'we'd
better get moving. The gates will be closed by the
time we get back, and there just happens to be a fine.'

'Oh, to hell with the fine,' she snapped, 'to hell
with the gates! I'm not interested.' Something
seemed to be breaking up inside her. 'I don't care
about the gates,' she said again.

'You don't care about anything, let's face it.' His
fingers dug into her shoulders as he turned her
round to face him. She gazed at him and he
returned her gaze, coolly, fixedly, not blinking, but
holding it intensely, interminably, until at last she
was forced to lower her lashes and then his mouth
was on hers. His hands, tanned and long-fingered,
possessed unexpected strength and, in the confined
area, he held her close. He kissed her with an
almost brutal intensity, his mouth biting into her

own. Tirza was powerless to stop her mouth from answering his and she satisfied the longing she had to touch the hard skin beneath his shirt, opening his shirt so that she could feel more of his body against her own. She freed her lips from his so that she could kiss his chest, burying her face into the wiry hairs there. His fingers sought her chin and he turned her face upwards so that he could go on kissing her. She was only vaguely aware of the far-back cry of some animal and her world had narrowed down to nothing more but the hard, close circle of Hugo's arms.

He released her suddenly, and she stared at him with eyes that were a little out of focus. Humiliated, she said, 'I think you are detestable!'

'If you think that you'd have stopped me,' his blue eyes went over her and she tried to slap his face, but he caught her wrist. 'I'm warning you, if you try that again, Miss Harper, I may just re-taliate, and you seem hellbent on discovering this for yourself.'

'I'll try it, anyway,' she told him, watching him as he got out of the car.

'I'll follow you,' he called out, not looking at her.

They reached the camp to find the gates had been closed by the black game guards. With their slouch hats and khaki uniforms they appeared efficient and polite, and Tirza, watching Hugo pay the fine, felt young and lonely—and ridiculous.

'Okay,' he said, coming towards the Alfa-Romeo, 'you know where to park my car.'

She sat in hostile silence, staring up at him, and

then she set the car in motion and drove in the direction of the bungalows.

Without waiting for him, she got out of the car and ran up the steps to her bungalow, and at the sight of the golden thatched room and twin beds, covered with golden-yellow covers, she felt an urge to collapse and never get up again. She felt nervously drained and exhausted.

A moment later Hugo was at her door. 'Please be ready to dine at the restaurant.' His eyes went over her. 'There'll be time for you to slip under a shower, if you like.'

'I have no wish to dine,' she said, assessing his masculinity as he stood there, looking at her.

'Don't be ridiculous,' he said.

'I'm not being ridiculous. I loathe you. I loathe the lot of you, and I have no wish to eat in your company.'

'That doesn't worry me. Anyway, honesty is better than lying,' he told her. 'You're improving.'

'Thank you,' she said sarcastically.

'Before we eat, however,' he went on, 'I'm going to buy you a drink.'

'I said no! Leave me alone and get back to your lady-friend and her mother.'

'They're included in the invitation,' he said.

Pointedly, Tirza moved towards the shower-cubicle and was shocked when his hand shot out and he grasped her wrist. His fingers were hard and unyielding.

'You'll do as I say.'

'How do you profess to *make* me?' She was furious now. 'How? Just tell me that?'

'I've had some experience in making women do things they don't want to do. Don't provoke me, Tirza.'

After a moment she said, 'Damn you and your insufferable air of superiority!' She was feeling angrier than she had ever felt in her life.

Wearing cream slacks and a spice-brown body-shirt, which she left daringly unbuttoned, to match the mood she was in, and several strands of pink pearls, she waited tensely in her bungalow until she felt it was time to join the others outside.

There was an awkward pause when she did, but Cathy broke it by saying, with a slight pursing of her lips, 'Isn't it a heavenly night? Hungry, Tirza?'

Tirza felt stunned—just as though nothing had happened to cause the ill-feeling which was nothing short of potent. I'm not letting her get away with that, she thought.

'I could ask you the same question, Cathy.' There was a wealth of meaning in the tone of her voice.

'I asked first,' Cathy laughed lightly, but there was tension in the sound.

'Well, no, Cathy, as a matter of fact I'm not hungry,' Tirza replied coldly.

'A drink will soon put that right,' Hugo cut in. 'Let's go.' He was the type of man who became impatient when women kept him waiting and was used to putting an end to it by handing out orders.

They walked the short distance to the magnificently constructed restaurant of stone, thatch and wooden beams, which blended so perfectly with the surroundings.

Over drinks, which they had in the tremendous lounge, conversation was stilted. Dinner was not what could be described as a pleasant meal. There was too much of an atmosphere and, into the bargain, the air-conditioning was turned up to its highest, and Tirza felt herself shivering. Deliberately, however, she left the warming liquid in her glass untouched.

When she was back in her bungalow, she heaved a sigh of relief. Her whole visit to Swaziland had been distorted by the two women her father had introduced into her life.

Before getting into bed she went to check the latch on the screened door to the veranda, for there was no key to her room. The latch on the door was broken and although, in the Game Reserve, latches and locks were of little concern this added to her tense and unhappy state.

Outside, the sky was restless with glittering stars and somewhere close by a wild dog barked, and the bark ended in a wild yap, yap, yapping, increasing in volume when more dogs joined in. The camp, however, was very quiet, with the people who had dined in the restaurant either in bed or preparing for it. All that mattered in this part of the world was a good night's rest, after an exciting day of game-spotting and who was going to be the first out of the gates at sunrise for more game-spotting. The glowing fires where people had grilled meat over charcoal had practically died out.

Having no key and a broken latch bugged her. After all, she was alone in the bungalow. Cathy had Paige and Paige had Cathy, and Hugo was all arrogant male. She felt tired, emotionally and physically drained, and it was not surprising, therefore, that she had the recurrent dream.

The bird was there, but she couldn't see it, and it cried ... pea-or, pea-or! It was a cry which seemed to underline her terrible loneliness and, in the dream, she felt her hands shaking and her heart beating so fast that it seemed to be choking her. 'It's only a peacock,' D.H. was saying, 'darling, it's only a peacock ... a peacock in the jungle.' Something had changed that jungle, though. Once it had been the enchanted Indian background of her very early childhood with leaves and flowers and brightly coloured birds and sunset skies. Now, however, there was no sign of her mother. She had gone, gone ... pea-or, pea-or ...

When Hugo gathered her in his arms she was still screaming in that thin, eerie manner.

'Oh, no,' she began to sob now, shaking her head, from side to side. 'Oh, no, no ...' Her voice rose, as she clung to him, trying to focus her eyes on his face.

'Tirza! What is it?' She could make him out in the moonlight which flooded her bungalow. 'You should have drawn your curtains,' he was saying, as he stroked her hair back from her face. 'Moonlight does the craziest things to one's sleep.'

Tirza made the transition from sleep to total wakefulness.

'I wanted to be able to see out—to see your bungalow. I was—frightened,' she told him.

'You should have told me.' His voice was abrupt. 'Why didn't you tell me you were nervous?'

Sitting up, she asked, 'How did you hear me? Was I *that* loud?' She felt acutely embarrassed now.

'As I remarked, moonlight does the craziest things to one's sleep. I couldn't sleep and went to sit outside at the garden table, in front of my bungalow, and then I heard this—this haunting thread of sound . . . you have no idea . . . what were you dreaming about, to make you sound like that?' He slid his hand up from her tense shoulder to the back of her neck, beneath her hair.

'It's just a dream I have, from time to time, especially if I happen to be overtired, or run down. I know it sounds crazy, but I call it my peacock in the jungle dream.' Her face reflected the silver of the night.

'Is there any reason why you should have this dream?' he asked. He moved his hand gently against her neck and then his fingers went to her hair.

'Because we lived in India, I guess. At one stage I remember this kind of faded, pink-washed bungalow—you see, I was very young and it's sort of confused—with faded pink-washed walls all around it. You could hear them crying, somewhere out in what could be described as a jungle. They—that sound—was all that was left after my mother died . . . I always seem to have this dream, which never differs, when I'm particularly upset or fatigued.'

'Were you feeling this way tonight?'

'Yes.' She lifted a hand and took his fingers from her hair. 'What do *you* think? If I could have got out of coming here with you, I would have, believe me.'

· Feeling childish and vulnerable, now, because of the dream and the screaming which had gone along with it, she tossed the bedclothes to one side and slipped her legs over the side of the bed and stood up in one fluid movement.

She began searching around for her gown which she appeared to have mislaid. She was wearing a man's fine cotton shirt, exotically striped in purple, crimson, dark-blue and honey, and she looked like a stylised fashion model. The lines of her body were long, although she was not tall. In the moonlight, her face, tawny hair and skin seemed to have no colour except a hint of pale bronze. She turned, suddenly, and looked at Hugo. 'Where's my gown?' she asked, feeling confused and thankful, at the same time—for she was wearing bikini briefs beneath the shirt.

It had slipped on to the floor and he found it for her and then, wide-eyed, she watched him as he came towards her. Her huge green eyes went on gazing at his face as he draped the garment about her slim shoulders. She could feel the weight of his look on her lips, her throat and her bosom and then dropping to her bare legs. Her lashes went down as he sought her mouth with his own and she heard the catch of her own breath when he possessed her breast and the caressing movement of his fingers warmed the response in her. As he sought her, more and more, she knew that tonight there was no question, and she moved against him eagerly, ignited by his touch, the feel of his hard body against her own. There was no protest as he began to undo the buttons of the shirt. Expertly he drew out her feelings, and then, bringing her to her senses, he said, 'There's no need for you to turn your feline wiles on me, Tirza. I guess I can supply the details you're craving for your weaving industry, without any favours from you. You appear to have got over your nightmare now.'

She stood staring back at him and her face was appalled. 'You devil,' she told him. 'You ... *devil*, devil, devil! I hate you! Get out! You're—you're like those predators, out there, beyond the fence ... ruthless and cruel. Why don't you tear this contract up and let me go?'

'Because I happen to be a business man,' he told her.

After he had gone, the silence of her bungalow was enough to remind her how acutely she had wanted Hugo to possess her. She was plunged into depression. Later, there were the usual animal night-noises to unnerve her as she lay awake ... the cough, cough of a lion, before it roared somewhere out there beyond the security fence of the camp, the silly nerve-chilling laughter of a hyena.

Eventually, however, all thought went from her and she dozed, and the sun was not yet up when she was awake again.

CHAPTER SIX

THE sky was flushed a dark crimson and Tirza slipped from her bed and shrugged into her gown, then went out to the small screened veranda, enjoying the cool air for a few moments.

Then she took a shower and, by this time, Cathy and Paige had set out coffee cups on one of the garden tables outside the bungalows.

'It makes such a difference starting the day with nice cup of coffee,' Cathy was saying, 'before going along to the restaurant for breakfast. Good morning, Tirza. Sleep well?'

For Hugo's benefit Tirza replied coldly, 'I'll do us both a favour, Cathy, by not answering that question.'

Beyond the lawns, planted trees and shrubs, the bush started in earnest with just the high protecting fence to act as barrier against wild animals. Birds were twittering and there were sounds of people preparing to go out in cars to spot game.

Hugo did not eat breakfast in the restaurant and left, soon after drinking his coffee, for the rest camp at Letaba, where apparently he had a business appointment in connection with orders for the curio and gift shops there.

During breakfast Paige's face took on a mean look. 'Tirza,' she said, 'that was a corny thing to do—telling Hugo that your name was Theron. You

107

might have known it would have to come out in casual conversation.'

Shaking out a soft caftan which was created from mohair and bowed to the Middle East for style, Tirza answered her shortly. 'My name does just happen to be Tirza Theron Harper, Paige, believe it or not.'

Cathy cut in swiftly, 'We just happened to be speaking about Harper's, Tirza, that's all.'

'It doesn't matter,' Tirza kept her voice neutral, 'I really don't want to talk about this. In any case, once this is over, I won't be seeing Hugo Harrington again. It's neither here nor there, when you work it all out.'

'When you work it all out,' Paige drawled, 'it was a lousy thing to do ... coming to Swaziland to crib ideas for your own weaving industry.'

'That's a disgusting lie! However, so far as I'm aware, Paige, there's no law about how many weaving industries there are in a country. In any case, you paint a far worse picture than it was supposed to be. You and your mother blew the entire thing up—out of all proportion. Why didn't you tackle me first? Why did you have to run to him with tales, like a couple of children? I could have explained so much, given half a chance.' Her throat tightened up. 'Crib is a hard word, you know. I came to buy for Harper's and merely to look around. I'm not the deceitful person you imagine me to be.'

Hugo was not present at the two fashion shows, which took place in the restaurant and which took place without a hitch. Tirza and the Mobrays endured one another, speaking with politeness and even consideration. After all, they had a job to do. Hugo had, in fact, gone into the bush with two game rangers in a Land Rover. Tirza realised that he was not the type of man to get involved with this part of his business and, quite apart from that, there was an abrasiveness about him that went along with his unwillingness to suffer the moods of women, whether one of them happened to be his girl-friend or not.

He arrived back towards sunset, looking even more tanned and wearing denim wranglers, tight across his narrow hips. His shirt had been left unbuttoned, practically to the waist, because of the heat, and the cuffs were turned back to his elbows. Looking at him, Tirza suddenly felt clear-headed and exhilarated because he was back. This was ridiculous, she knew, for he had given her only a casual glance upon arrival, and before going into his bungalow.

The breeze brought with it sweet, spicy and animal scents and, in the sinking sunlight, the bungalows looked almost pink.

Over dinner, which they had at the restaurant, Tirza plucked up enough courage to say, 'By the way, would it be possible for me to be dropped off somewhere tomorrow? You know—at one of the small towns just outside the reserve where I can get a train to the Karroo, or catch a flight. You see, I'm going to my father's farm for a while.' Now that she had decided, she felt suddenly very calm. Her green eyes rested on Hugo's face.

When he answered her his voice was nothing but

polite. 'We can arrange something, I'm sure. I'll
work it out, don't worry.'

'Thank you.' Her voice was expressionless.

'Will somebody be expecting you at the farm?'
Cathy asked, but it seemed obvious that she had
asked the question because, as the woman Douglas
Harper had nearly married, this was expected of
her.

'Gerry and Zelma Strauss will be there. Gerry is
manager there.' There was an edge to Tirza's
voice.

'Oh yes.' Cathy lifted her glass to her lips, and
Tirza was quick to notice that her hand was
shaking.

For a giddy moment Tirza felt like spilling the
beans about Cathy and her father, but thought
better of it. There was a haughty look about her,
almost, as she looked directly at Cathy. She was
thinking that although Cathy might have stooped
to carrying tales she had not yet reached that
stage.

They left the camp before the sun was up the
following morning and then, scarlet and huge and
smudged with early-morning mist, it slid up and
over the horizon. In the foreground, the trees
looked like black lacework which was being lit up,
from behind, by a huge scarlet globe.

Paige had looked mean and spiteful at the discovery that Tirza was once again to travel with
Hugo in his car, while she and Cathy headed back
for Swaziland to manage the boutique there.

It was a balmy morning, but there was the usual
threat of intense heat. From the car they saw

giraffe, zebra and impala, not to mention a herd of elephants, and any conversation which took place between Hugo and herself revolved around the animals.

Some time later, when game was scarce, Hugo said coldly, 'By the way, did you really think I would dump you in some little town to find your own way to the Karroo?'

With an odd little thrill she said, 'That was the arrangement, wasn't it? You said you would arrange to do this.'

'I said that something could be arranged. This is the something. I'll take you to the farm in the Karroo.'

'Thank you. That's very kind of you,' she murmured, while relief surged through her.

He went on, 'We'll stop at a roadhouse for breakfast and again, possibly at a motel, for lunch, then we'll probably stop over somewhere for the night.' He turned to look at her. 'Right?'

'Yes, of course. Present speed restrictions make it impossible to cover great distances.'

'We'll leave for the farm in the morning.'

'Fine.' Tirza stared through the windscreen, dreading the moment when Hugo would walk out of her life.

In the afternoon a violent thunderstorm struck the countryside with ferocity, spilling rain over everything and bending trees. The sky was veined by lightning and the windscreen wipers hardly coped with the blinding rain.

Hugo turned off the National Road, which was running with water, and Tirza noticed the country hotel. There were a number of other cars parked beneath the trees, in front of reception, including two familiar-looking Land Rovers. Hugo parked the car and turned to look at her. 'I know you happen to enjoy nature's pyrotechnics, but driving in this is beyond a joke. This will just have to do.'

'It—it looks very nice,' she stammered, 'what you can see of it.'

He came round to her side and opened the door for her and they ran through the rain to the steps which led on to a wide patio. Two enormous wild fig trees shuddered in the wind and showered more rain over them and, laughing lightly, they were almost blown into the foyer.

Purple bougainvillaea, which had been whisked in by the wind, scudded across a black and white tiled floor and two huge dogs rushed towards Tirza in friendly greeting.

Shaking back her wet hair, Tirza patted them while Hugo made the necessary arrangements at the desk.

Her room was next to his and there was a view of the swimming-pool and, because of the rain, the water appeared grey and uninviting.

After settling in, they went through to the lounge, and from where they sat, they could see the foyer and the reception desk, through a wide arch. It was almost dark now and the wind and the rain seemed to have gone mad. Eventually the glass doors to the foyer were closed, blocking out the rain and wind.

Tirza was conscious of Hugo's eyes watching her and she tried to conceal her uncertainty under a slightly nonchalant air, but this uncertainty was shortlived when two game rangers sauntered up to the table and joined them for drinks. The strain of eating dinner, alone with Hugo, was also broken when the four of them shared a table. Tirza was now able to account for the Land Rover which was parked outside and which had seemed familiar to her, somehow.

Hugo seemed in no mood for her company and she left him at the pub with the rangers, and as she prepared for bed she found herself wondering how cruel Hugo Harrington could be to a woman ... and just how kind. After a considerable time lag, thinking about these things, and in which she lay waiting for sleep to overtake her, it did, and when she awoke it was morning.

After breakfast, again at the table for four, they left for the farm; Hugo had little to say, and Tirza was determined not to be the one to volunteer conversation.

They lunched high up on the patio of a country hotel which overlooked poplar trees and valleys. In the distance, the koppies blurred to a pale pink and rose in strange and grotesque shapes. In a fenced-in area of the gardens there were sleek golden buck and some ostriches. To one side of the area white walls enclosed a garden where peacocks strutted about. Tirza glanced quickly in Hugo's direction, as memory flooded her being, and when their eyes met she was startled by the expression in his and looked away.

'Somewhere out there, and beneath those koppies, which either appear pink or mauve from a distance, is my father's farm,' she said.

'That must excite you,' he replied, almost carelessly.

For a moment she asked herself whether she should try to explain everything to him, but his brusquerie warned her not to say anything.

A pink organdie cloth, adrift with sprays of white blossom and green leaves, and napkins to match, billowed out from the round table. Venetian wine goblets glittered in the sunlight which filtered through the branches of a tree growing in the centre of the patio. Without any sign of bad weather, it was a romantic setting. Hugo was wearing beige slacks which accentuated his maleness, and a darker beige shirt, open at the neck, as usual.

'W—when we leave here, would you like me to drive?' Tirza asked.

'Would you like to drive?' He gave her a sudden, contagious smile.

'Would *you* like me to?' she asked, flustered.

'Oblige me by answering my question,' he snapped, and she realised that she had been a fool to be taken in by that smile. She met his eyes with her wide stare. Who did he think he was? she asked herself. His peremptoriness angered her. 'I thought it would give you a break,' she told him, 'and yes, I would like to drive.'

'Fine,' he replied, and then surprised her when he went on, 'When we part, it won't be with assurance of future meetings, and yet we'll probably meet again one day . . . in Cape Town. I suppose you'll commute between the Karroo and Cape Town?'

'Yes—I—er—suppose so . . . I will commute, of course.' Her voice was sober.

The organdie cloth billowed out from the table and she caught it with her slender fingers and held it down. Her lacquered nails were the same fragile pink as the cloth, her eyes the same colour as the leaves which were sprigged upon the material.

Wheeling a white wrought-iron trolley with rubber tires, a waiter came towards them. Tirza glanced at the superb assortment of cheeses and biscuits but said, 'No, thank you.' Her golden-tanned face blended with her tawny hair, which seemed to be streaked with silver—the result of long hours in the sun, sea and pool.

'You've barely eaten,' Hugo commented.

For the benefit of the waiter she smiled, 'No, really, I couldn't possibly eat any more.'

They went out to the car and he handed her the keys. 'Driving this car is nothing new to you, after all,' he said, 'but take it easy.'

Once again he seemed moodily preoccupied, and Tirza wondered whether he was thinking of Paige, who would probably be back in Swaziland by now, and the thought caused her to feel jealous.

Hugo's car handled well and telegraph poles slid by, along with motionless windmills. Once, as she slackened speed until it was safe to overtake another vehicle, she noticed a rock-rabbit, sitting on a boulder. His whiskers twitched nervously, but he made no move to run and, on the spur of the moment, Tirza called out, 'Hi there!'

'A relative of yours?' Hugo sounded amused.

'Yes. How did you guess?' The vastness soothed

her, the wonderful sense of space and those wispy clouds hanging over three high koppies which were hunched together.

'Talking about relations,' she said, feeling suddenly relaxed with Hugo, 'don't those three koppies look like relations, hunched together, for comfort?'

When he made no reply she felt affronted and put her foot down harder on the accelerator.

Sheep grazed behind fences and tall sisals flourished around a farm with a dam and dried mealie stalks. The farmhouse was ugly and looked desolate in the hot sun, and she found herself wondering what Hugo was going to think of her father's farm.

The windows of the car were down and the wind blew her hair about her face. Her eyes flickered to the dashboard and she saw she was breaking the speed limit, but the road was a ribbon and she felt suddenly reckless. Beside her, Hugo's dark blue eyes regarded her with a speculative interest, but he did not speak.

Fir trees cast shade where shade was needed on yet another farm in this semi-desert like land. Wild scrub grew to look as if it was planned to grow that way. Horses looked over a gate. Fences appeared like man-made spider webs, glinting in the sun. For a moment Tirza slackened speed because she was approaching a settlement spread beneath a lone koppie which looked like a pyramid, and to one side of the koppie a Mexican-shaped cactus was absolutely striking in its isolation—like a sculpture, she found herself thinking idly.

Something told her that Hugo was becoming angry at the way in which she was driving, and this provoked her into going faster. 'Look at that train,' she said. 'It looks like logs on wheels, doesn't it? Or a child's toy.'

'You should know,' he said, 'since you're acting like a damned child.'

'Are you afraid?' she laughed. 'Afraid I might wreck your Alfa-Romeo? It could have been wrecked, if those elephants had charged at the waterhole.'

'Do it your own way,' he said sarcastically. 'You're a remarkable girl, after all, Miss Harper.'

The countryside was so barren, but strangely beautiful, the koppies and pale gold grasses catching the sun which was beginning to slant now. The distant koppies were drawing closer, drawing in, forming a circle. Windmills, bridges and dry river beds flashed by. Muddy dams and mirages danced wildly. Farm graveyards, with elaborate headstones which had baked all day beneath the sun— having baked there for generations, in some cases—had a forlorn look about them ... They were nearly there.

And then she was being flagged down by two traffic policemen who signalled for her to stop and to pull over on to the side of the road.

'Now talk your way out of this one, Miss Harper, if you can.' Hugo gave her a sarcastic excuse of a smile and folded his arms.

Furious and humiliated, Tirza reversed back to where the officers had stationed themselves. The man who spoke to her had a face that was almost austere.

'Uu-uh,' he said, shaking his head and looking almost sad. 'Uu-uh, we can't allow that. We've got a speed check, and you hit this point at a cool hundred and twenty plus, but we won't go into that, right now.

Answering with some heat, she said, 'I think it's unfair!' She was acutely aware of Hugo just sitting there, looking almost bored. 'How awful to hide here in the thorn bushes on a National Road which, because of its very isolation, is almost deserted.'

'So you think it's unfair, hey?' The policeman took out a notebook and his face was set in an expression of total hostility now as he lifted his lashes to give her a long look. 'Ever heard of the oil crisis?'

Moodily she watched him write the date on the form.

'We get too much of this sort of thing on the roads,' the officer continued, 'and that's why we trap where we do, like this, with our vehicles and ourselves hidden from the road—until it's too late. That's not being unfair.' He glanced accusingly across at Hugo. 'We have to stamp this sort of thing out, sir.'

'Don't worry,' Hugo voice was hard. 'The young lady's father will come to light with the fine.'

'Who pays up is not my concern,' the officer replied coldly, handing Tirza the ticket. 'Good day to you.'

When they were alone Hugo said, 'Serves you

right. So? So—we all take chances in life. Who doesn't? But you were chewing up those kilometres like they were going out of fashion. What the devil got into you?'

His male superiority aggravated her and she retorted hotly, 'I'm naturally reckless.'

'Yes, so I'd noticed, right from the beginning—as far back as the Eastern Boulevard, as a matter of fact. Okay, Tirza, shift over. I'll drive the rest of the way.'

He got out of the car and came round to the driver's side and with an impatient breath she slipped across to the passenger seat, where she sat in hostile silence. All she wanted was to obliterate the whole wretched scene and undo all that she had said and done, leading up to this very moment.

At the familiar turn-off a field of wild flowers made a splash of colour, defying the heat and the dryness.

'Turn left,' she said, a fresh surge of humiliation washing over her, 'and you'd better slacken off.'

Hugo laughed at that, turning to look at her. He provoked in her a desire to lash out at him.

Unlike some Karroo gates that collapse in a muddle of poles and clanking wire the moment they are opened, the gates to Douglas Harper's farm were imposing. In the distance the farmhouse was surrounded by tall stately poplar trees and the area was green and lush, like an oasis, and the sight of it caused Tirza to bite into her lip in the pain she felt.

She was aware of Hugo's eyes taking in the

beautiful garden and lawns and Karroo fruit
trees—plums, apricots, figs, quinces and pome-
granates. Surrounding all this were the type of
farmlands where merino sheep and black-headed
Persians thrive, and it was a part of the country
where the price of wool was always the topic of
conversation when people managed to get together.
And then, when he saw the house, white and huge,
with tremendous windows, with the panes set in
small white squares, he whistled very softly.

'So this is what you have in mind. Yes, I can see
it all . . . I hand it to you. Quite a shrewd business
woman. It's an ideal spot for a thriving weaving
industry.'

'Yes, isn't it?' Her voice was like ice. 'And yes
again. I am a shrewd business woman. In fact, an
independent eccentric, like my father.'

'Shall I park beneath the pillared portico, where
there appears to be room for three more cars?' he
asked, with heavy sarcasm.

'Yes. Actually there happens to be room for *four*
more cars, Mr Harrington. You're slipping up on
your calculations.'

'I'll try to not feel thrown off balance about it.'
He dismissed her remark with a casual shrug.

With its carriage lights on either side of the
magnificently carved door, the house looked more
like a hotel, which, of course, it used to be.

'Some farmhouse,' Hugo commented. 'It must
be the only one like it in the entire semi-desert. It's
always been obvious to me, of course, that your
father . . . D.H., as you refer to him . . . does
everything on a grand scale, like his independent

daughter here, who has all the ability necessary to make a stage of every place she happens to be in.'

Suddenly Tirza felt the need to explain. 'It used to be a hotel,' she said. 'It even had a liquor licence. My father bought it because it adjoined those farmlands out there, and he had it converted and modernised and here it stands.' Her voice was abrupt. 'Empty and waiting for someone to come along and enjoy it. Usually, but not so far as this farm is concerned, my father simply telephones ahead, alerts his staff and one of his homes is immediately brought to life. However, although nobody has been alerted now there's a small staff, nevertheless, behind that koppie over there, and Delphina and her husband are in a cottage, at the back of this house. I have my own key, though. I have keys to all the houses my father owns, of course. Gerry Strauss, my father's manager, has his own very attractive house, which you could see from the gates. It's beside that other koppie over there. I'll fix you a drink and find you something to eat and, with the memory of my future weaving industry to haunt you, you can be on your way.'

'We'll drive to Gerry's place first,' he said.

'Why?' She gave him a direct look.

Shrugging carelessly, he said, 'To find out if he's there, so that you won't be alone here. It's just that old chivalry in me coming out—this inclination I have to defend a girl in distress. You must have noticed that on the night that we met on the Eastern Boulevard.'

'I'm anything but distressed,' she lied.

'You will be, if you suddenly discover that Gerry

Strauss and his wife have gone off somewhere and you find yourself alone here.'

'Being alone doesn't worry me. I'm often alone.'

'Well, I'm not leaving you alone here.' His voice conveyed authority. 'Let's go. How do you get round that koppie, anyway? Does there happen to be a road, or a track?'

'Oh, come on! Not a *track*. There's a road, well surfaced, perfect . . . like everything else you see.'

As they drove round the koppie there was a tall, shady tree, where merino sheep and goats were drinking from a trough to which an outlet pipe was connected.

'Well, the animals are home,' Hugo cast her an amused glance. 'I guess that's always something, and you do, after all, have an interest in the angora goats.'

'At least they're polite,' Tirza replied tartly.

Gerry Strauss was on the veranda and for a moment, he looked puzzled, then he stood up and came down the steps.

'Well, surprise, surprise!' he came towards Tirza. His eyes flickered in Hugo's direction and Tirza said,

'I'd like you to meet Hugo Harrington, Gerry. He's on his way to Cape Town and gave me a lift here. We just wanted to make sure that you and Zelma were here, before he leaves.'

'Zelma's not here, I'm afraid. You see,' Gerry flushed slightly, 'there's going to be a baby and she's gone away for a few days, for the usual check-up. She stays with her mother.'

'Oh, that's super! I'm so glad.' Tirza did her best to sound cheerful.

Gerry glanced to the beer mug on a glass-topped cane table. 'I was enjoying a beer. What can I offer you?'

'We haven't come to stay,' Tirza said quickly. 'In fact, I haven't even let Delphina know that I'm here.'

'There's always something to eat at your father's house,' said Gerry, 'but everything will be in the deep freeze. Look, I'll send you a couple of steaks and some milk, how's that?' He glanced at Hugo. 'Tirza can organise a bit for you before you get on your way.'

'Fine.' There was a quirk to Hugo's mouth. 'A bite would always be appreciated.'

'And, by the way, your father's cellar is always well stocked, as you know,' Gerry added. 'Okay, be seeing you, Tirza. Cheerio . . .' His eyes brushed Hugo.

When they were passing the merino sheep and goats drinking at the trough beneath the big tree Hugo said, 'You'd better come on to Cape Town with me.'

'Why?' Tirza's eyes widened, as she turned to look at him.

'Well, you're sufficiently beautiful for his wife to be jealous if she comes back to find you here, alone with her husband.'

Turning on him furiously, she began to defend herself. 'In a completely different house? I don't intend moving into Gerry's house, dammit! Besides, there are other people here . . . you're insulting!'

'I'm being realistic,' he replied easily.

'You depress me,' she murmured.

'So will she be, if she comes back to find you here.' Suddenly he laughed. 'I'm telling you this as a friend.'

'Oh, dry up!' She turned away from him.

He parked the car and then followed her into the high-ceilinged Italian-tiled entrance hall. There were dried hydrangeas on an antique chest, which Tirza had put there on the last visit to the farm with her father. The flowers still managed to look attractively burnished, but then she had treated them. The Persian carpet on the floor still had that new smell about it.

'This is a carved bridal chest, by the way,' Tirza told him in a brittle voice. 'It waits, in vain, for the bride who never came. It's eighteenth century, I believe. Tch, tch! So sad. Through here . . .' She led the way through double white-panelled doors into the richly coloured lounge which was huge and beamed and very beautiful.

'And this is the drawing-room, you might say, also waiting for people who never come or, at the very least, seldom come.' Now that she had actually met the woman who had let her father down she was filled with bitterness.

'Why are you saying all this?' Hugo snapped. 'You can't be in every home at one time.'

'I wasn't thinking of me, as it so happens.' Her voice was unsteady.

The gold carpeting was thickly piled and topped by more Persian rugs with a ruby-red background and the curtains at the impressive windows were bronze shantung. Low, low sofas, upholstered in bronze, yellow and green floral linen, flanked a white fireplace, on either side of which were built-in alcoves, ducoed white, and housing blue-and-white Delft china. A collection of brass and copper gleamed and indicated that Delphina was giving careful attention to looking after the mansion. There were no fresh flowers in the room, but a huge copper fire-screen provided the necessary interest. An original Tinus de Jongh painting hung over the white fireplace.

Hugo went to stand at one of the long windows that overlooked a cobalt-blue swimming-pool, with boulder-backed ornamental walls, to provide shelter from the Karroo wind, tall cacti and white urns spilling out magenta bougainvillaea. Beyond, there was a superb view of those strange koppies and dry-looking but succulent bushes in the semi-desert-like land which stretched away to more mauve-hazed koppies.

Looking at him, Tirza knew the need to be sarcastic again. He was also so quick to judge her on her father's money.

'If you want to use a——' she pronounced it *ay*—'bathroom there are five to choose from. You can take your choice.' She smiled a radiant, meaningless smile that showed neither warmth nor relation to the bitterness behind her words. 'There used to be eleven bathrooms and eleven toilets—by hotel standards, it wasn't large, by any means, of course. Many rooms were broken down to enlarge others. You'll find everything to be above average size, of course. My father had it all going for him, with a prominent architect working out the necessary alterations. Of course, the architect took certain liberties—like creating a movie set, for instance.'

'You don't have to impress me,' he said. 'I'm sure it will all make an excellent background to what you've earmarked it to be. The colour of the tiles, wallpaper, the size of the rooms and the view makes no difference to me.'

Suddenly he closed the distance between them and caught her in his arms, and before she could stop him, he kissed her with almost savagery, then held her back to say, 'It's a pity you didn't get to find out what it was you wanted to know about what goes into starting a weaving industry in Swaziland, isn't it? Still, now that we've got this far—to the actual site, as it were, perhaps we can begin to work things out, to our mutual interest. What do you say? You give me what *I* want and I'll give you what you want.'

'Let go of me!' she snapped, resisting him. 'Don't think you're unique, with your weaving industry and your boutiques and those orders from the reserve . . . you're not, and what's more I . . .'

'Shut up!' Hugo muttered, his mouth fastening on to her own. For a moment she went on struggling and then, all at once, the resistance and rigidity drained from her and the ground seemed no longer to be solid beneath the sandals she was wearing.

His lips were cool and firm and his kisses were slow-moving, now, depriving her of all power of thought.

When he released her she stared at him. 'What am I supposed to do,' her breath was coming fast, 'go down on my knees and say thank you?'

She found herself running from the room and when she reached the bedroom, which was supposed to be hers but which felt like a place on the moon to her, she knew that she was shaking beyond belief. Suddenly she felt terrifyingly alone. Crossing the pale willow-leaf green carpet, she went into the bathroom and splashed her face. Here again everything was sheer, expensive luxury, and she gazed at the floor and walls of pink-veined marble, delicate jade-green marble sunken bath and gold dolphin taps, the glittering array of crystal bottles and jars on heavy glass shelves, awaiting her use, and the fluffy jade and pink towels.

'All you've ever thought about is money!' she said aloud. 'Money, money, money. Meetings, travelling to far-distant places. D.H., what have you *done* to me?' She gave way to wild sobbing, swallowing and gulping and clenching her fingers. Then she calmed down and splashed her face and repaired the damage caused by tears.

The clothes hanging in the built-in cupboards with their antique-white louvred doors were strangers to her, although she had worn them before. She remembered how she had had a row with D.H. the day before they left the farm and how she had not even bothered to pack. She had simply walked out and left the clothes behind and, what was more staggering, she had not even missed them.

When she joined Hugo in the beamed lounge she was wearing a white, sleeveless dress which accentuated her tan and the slimness of her. Her hair had been scraped to the top of her head, where it was caught by a large tortoiseshell slide.

Going in the direction of the drinks cabinet, she said elaborately, 'Let me fix you a drink, before your meal.'

'Let me do it.' He came to stand beside her and his eyes went over her face. 'You've been crying.'

'Well, yes! What do you expect?'

'You're nursing a sense of humiliation, because you responded.' There was a compelling intensity in his dark blue eyes.

'I am humiliated, yes. For once, you're right.' She stood to one side, watching him as he poured their drinks with flamboyant skill.

Something got the better of her and she suddenly wanted him to know about this house and who was behind the planning of it. 'Do you know,' she pronounced each word very carefully, because she felt like crying again, 'at the time . . .' she stopped to gain control of herself, 'at the time, I wondered why D.H. was buying a farm—I mean—*a farm*? I wondered about the alterations to this place. He furnished with such care, but I guess you can see that for yourself?'

'Oh yes,' he passed her the glass and she took it carefully, determined not to touch his fingers, 'I noticed this same particular flair in the Bishopscourt mansion. I should imagine they're all like this—all the Harper homes. You sound so bitter when you talk about it—but don't worry, Tirza, I happen to like an organised environment.' She noticed the humourless quirk to his mouth.

'The last of the big spenders has nothing on my

father.' She took a sip of her drink, to calm her
nerves, and her taste buds cringed and she began
to cough and then she went on, 'Even I wondered
what D.H. was going to do with a sheep ranch.'
Suddenly she laughed, and the sound was tinged
with hysteria.

'Apart from the store complexes, high-rise housing complexes, a chalet in the Berg, holiday home
at Plettenberg Bay and a Cape-style house in Cape
Town, you mean?' She knew he was goading her
on.

'Ah,' she said, on a long breath, and then took
another sip of her drink, 'dear Cathy *has* been busy,
hasn't she? Well, yes, apart from all that . . .'

At that moment Delphina, wearing a red and
white spotted *kopdoek* over her head, tapped on
the white panelled door. 'The meat is here now,'
she said. 'When shall I grill it, Miss Tirza?'

Tirza was pale under her tan. 'Thank you,' she
murmured. 'I'll be with you in a moment,
Delphina.'

Moodily, she watched Hugo as he poured himself another drink and then he dropped ice into the
glass.

'I've decided, after all, to go back to Cape Town
with you. After Delphina has prepared a grill for
us and I've tossed a salad and we've eaten it, we
can be on our way.' In spite of all that had
happened she wanted to be with him until the last
possible moment and the thought of staying on
here after he had gone filled her with despair.

'Fine,' he said, shrugging, 'but what's caused you
to change your mind?'

'I hadn't intended staying here. I made that up, in the reserve. I was sick of having you and the Mobray females watching me like three scientists. What I had in mind was for you to drop me off at Phalaborwa, or somewhere, where I could find my own way back to Cape Town. I was coming here at a later stage.' She put her glass down. 'I'm going to help Delphina now.'

There were two cooking and preparing areas, a pantry and a breakfast nook, and beneath an elm canopy there was a stainless steel hob and an eye-level oven on each side. This cooking area was supposed to be used by the lady of the house, but Cathy had changed her mind about marrying D.H. On the paved floor there were brightly woven rugs, bearing the Swazi Signature name, ironically enough.

There was no sign of Delphina, so she went out to the courtyard and through a white archway to where Delphina and her husband lived in a cottage. She smiled as Delphina's children appeared, to stand, timid and suspicious, in the doorway.

'Hullo,' she said. 'Where's your mother?' While she was speaking her eyes flickered over the light brown faces, and then she saw the mongrel at their feet. It stared at her with light amber eyes and gave a saliva-dripping low snarl. On an impulse she said, 'Hello, boy,' but at the back of her fluttering mind was the knowledge that this dog was going to bite her.

Even though she had been expecting it, when it came she was absolutely unprepared for it. She was aware that she had cried out.

It was a bad bite—she knew that. And then Delphina was screaming from the door while her husband pushed past her and made, kicking, for the dog.

'Oh!' Delphina started shrieking. 'This dog is very cheeky, Miss Tirza. I'm sorry. He has bitten *two* people now.'

Shocked beyond belief, Tirza said, 'It's all right, Delphina. It's not your fault.' There seemed to be a lot of blood and it was on her fingers where she had tried to close the wound, behind her knee, with them. 'Mr Strauss will know what to do.'

When she went back into the lounge Hugo, glass in hand, was still standing where she had left him, but he turned as she came into the room. He put his glass down and came over to her. 'What is it? Tirza, in God's name, what's happened to make you look like this?'

After a moment, in which she had moistened her dry mouth with the tip of her tongue, she said, 'I'm afraid you'll have to take me back to Gerry's house.' She had been holding her leg and when she took her fingers away they were covered in blood and she saw shock leap to his eyes. Then he took her fingers and held them, staring at them with something like horror.

'It's nothing,' she told him quickly. 'I've only been bitten by a dog.' She turned slightly so that she could show him her leg and when he saw it he said, 'Oh, my God. You've only been bitten by a dog! *Only?* That's the understatement of the year! This is something for a doctor, Tirza, not Gerry Strauss!'

'Gerry's a doctor,' she spoke with some impatience now. 'Gerry's a veterinary surgeon, in other words, quite apart from the fact that he happens to be my father's farm manager. He'll know what to do—and quickly.'

'I'm not taking you to a vet,' he said.

'A vet is a doctor,' she said, 'quickly. Don't argue with me—the blood is pouring from me, Hugo. Now is not the time to talk about it.'

'Where can I get something to tie round your leg until we get there?' he asked.

'There's a cabinet in the kitchen,' she told him, 'where the breakfast nook is. If I remember correctly, there should be new dish towels in there and clean, torn up sheets which Delphina uses when she irons.'

She was afraid to take her fingers from the gaping wound and was holding her leg when Hugo came back. Suffering now from reaction, she was silent while he bound the leg with a strip of sheeting and then she found herself swept up in his arms as he prepared to carry her to the car.

When he had got her settled he asked, 'Are you all right?'

'Yes.' She inclined her head, keeping her pain to herself with a kind of self-sufficient quality which stemmed from being very much alone. He held her hand all the way to Gerry's house as he drove.

Immediately Gerry Strauss saw the wound he said, 'Tirza, this is one hell of a bite. You know that? It's going to have to be stitched, I'm afraid. All right?'

'I know it's going to have to be stitched,' she

answered. Her face was deathly pale and she had begun to shake badly. She glanced at Gerry for reassurance and was very quiet while he stitched the torn leg, catching her breath a little.

'Okay?' Hugo went down on his heels beside her, sweeping back a curtain of her tawny hair.

'Yes, fine, thank you.' After a moment she said, 'Gerry—what about—rabies?'

'Look,' he said, 'put rabies out of your mind, Tirza.'

'But Delphina says I'm the second person the dog has bitten recently.'

'I'm going to cover you with antibiotics,' he told her.

'But how will you *know*?' Her voice was strained. 'The dog might be rabid. I can hardly believe that dog has been inoculated. Have you seen it? It's nothing but a cur. I can't think what she's doing with it.'

'Just you leave everything to me,' Gerry told her. 'Unfortunately, we have to wait fourteen days before we know the verdict.'

'Fourteen days?' she gasped. 'Oh no!'

'Look, I only say unfortunately because you're going to worry—not because I happen to think the dog is rabid. You're going to worry and I'm not going to be able to stop you, but try not to think about it. I'm certain everything is going to be okay.'

'And then?' Tirza was white to the lips.

'If the worst comes to the worst, which I'm certain it won't, you'll undergo a course of twenty-one injections.'

'I see.' Her hair slipped forward over her cheeks. 'Well, that's that, I guess. Will I have to stay here for that period?'

'I suggest you remain here until the stitches come out, anyway. You said you were staying, anyway, didn't you?'

'Yes,' she replied dully, 'I did.'

'That bite is in a difficult spot. The stitches are probably going to bother you.'

'Well, fine.' She stood up and Hugo's arms steadied her.

Gerry tried to make light of things. 'I'll bet this is not what you had in mind when you mentioned that a bite would be appreciated!' He glanced at Hugo. 'When I said that Tirza could organise a bite for you before you left, I didn't mean this. Didn't you get the steaks?' He laughed and then looked embarrassed.

'Quite a surgery you have here,' Hugo commented.

Gerry looked around. 'Well, yes, I guess you could say that. Just as well. Sometimes my work doesn't always revolve around animals. I'm often having to help out.'

In the car going back, Tirza said, 'You go on ahead. I'll stay here until I'm fit to make a plan about getting back to Cape Town. Perhaps my father will be back. He can come and collect me, if he is.' Her voice sounded small and lonely. Hugo's departure was going to be like a tolling bell in her heart.

There was a sudden silence, as though they had simultaneously run out of words, and then, not looking at her, he said, 'I'll be staying on.'

'But why? It's not necessary.' She made an attempt to control the surge of joy. 'I mean, why should you?'

'Just let's say it's a dumb decision on my part,' he spoke almost gently, however. 'Do you think I'd leave you like this?' He parked the car beneath the large pillared portico and looked at her for a moment, before getting out and coming round to her side so that he could help her.

The scent of eucalyptus leaves hung in the still air and it mingled with the perfume of double white petunias growing in a white urn. White petunias were used again and cascaded over tall urns on the long paved area in front of the huge windows and intricately carved door. The sky was a sheet of gloriously tinted gold and pink and the sun had gone. Delphina had turned on the lamps and the house was ready waiting . . .

'Okay,' said Hugo, after he had carried Tirza inside. 'Sit here and I'll get Delphina, and directly she's prepared your room you'll get into bed and stay there and start on the capsules Gerry has given you.'

While he was away Tirza sat with her leg outstretched and closed her eyes. Her head was swimming from shock, and yet she found herself thinking about the time she had come here with her father, just before she had met Nigel Wright. It seemed a hundred years ago. Her father had been in the planning stage of marrying Cathy and, even then, he had not thought fit to tell her about Cathy and Paige Mobray. On that occasion, her father

had invited friends along—Gilbert and Nancy
Winters and their son Paul, and she had known
that Paul had been invited along on purpose when
D.H. had said, 'Bring some pretty clothes along.
We'll probably entertain a lot, give a couple of
weekend parties, while we're there.' To satisfy him
she had, and then she had left most of them
behind—long and short skirts, jeans and shorts and
tops to go with all of them, caftans, undies and
sleepwear and, what was now a staggering thought,
she had not even missed them after she had got
home. Poor, spoilt little rich girl. Well, those
clothes, which she had left behind in a fit of anger,
would come in useful now, for she had packed very
little for her Swaziland trip. Those clothes were also
going to give Hugo Harrington something more to
think about, when she started wearing them.

He came back into the lounge with Delphina and
she opened her eyes. 'I have already prepared the
bed for you and your husband, Miss Tirza.
Everything is ready.'

For a moment Tirza was thrown off guard and
then she said, 'Not my husband, Delphina. Mr
Harrington will have the room opposite mine.'

'Oh, you are not married? I'm sorry, I
thought . . .' Delphina looked embarrassed.

'We're thinking about marriage,' Hugo told her,
and his eyes were amused. 'No problem.'

Tirza was in the kingsize bed with its satin-
quilted bedhead when he came to her room. 'As
Gerry said,' he gave her a smile, 'that was one hell
of a bite. You handled it well.'

'Thank you.' She was surprised at the tone of

his voice. There was a softness in his expression—a softness she hadn't suspected was there.

'Gerry is sending a doctor here in the morning. You're going to need a prescription,' he told her.

'Yes, I realise he gave me only enough pills for tonight. Anyway, thank you for—everything, Hugo. By the way, please feel free to help yourself to whatever you want. My father's bar is well stocked. Will you do that?'

'Frankly, I could do with a drink. I'll leave you— unless there's anything you want?'

'No—not now. Later. Delphina is going to cook for us now. I'd just like to rest. Okay?'

Delphina had removed the pale pink and green bedspread and placed it on a small stool at the foot of the bed. The only thing that went to indicate that the kingsize bed belonged to one person was the one satin-shaded lamp that stood on a low antique-white lacquered cabinet, on one side.

Tirza lay back and was aware of the dull throbbing that was setting in at the back of her leg. Delphina brought her a steak, chips and a salad, and the tray was on the lacquered cabinet when Hugo returned to her room.

His eyes went to her plate. 'So you've eaten?'

'Yes.' She moistened her lips, unsure of herself.

'How are you feeling?' he asked.

'Not too bad, considering.' She was wearing a pale apricot nightdress which, although sleeveless, with a low square neckline, was demure, and she saw his blue eyes go to it.

'Your room is like a flower garden,' he said.

'How many flagons of perfume do you go through a month?'

She saw he had been drinking. 'Oh,' she shrugged, laughing a little, 'like my Parisian sister I adore perfume, I guess. Don't you like it?'

'I didn't say that, did I? They say that French women wander, like tipsy bees, from blossom to blossom.' While he was speaking she was beginning to wonder, a little excitedly, what he would be like to kiss with the smell of whisky on his breath. 'Anyway,' he went on looking down at her, 'don't they say that the average man is fascinated by the seductive aura of a particular perfume?'

'You seem to know all about it?' Tirza bit her lip.

'Well, I purchase it, from time to time,' he replied carelessly, 'and that's what they tell me.'

Moodily, she watched him as he sat down on the mattress. 'That tiny gap between your two front teeth is very fascinating. Did you know that? It's just the kind of imperfection, in an otherwise beautiful woman, that can haunt a man's memory.' Suddenly his eyes hardened. 'But of course that gap has been written about before today.'

'I don't ask for publicity,' she said. 'In fact, I hate it.'

'Do you?' He went on regarding her. 'You look worried. Is it because you know I've had a few drinks? I was suffering from reaction too.' He laughed softly, 'But I don't have a drinking problem.' His eyes went on mocking her.

'I didn't say you did.'

After a moment, to break the silence, Tirza went on talking. 'I'll have to phone my father, of course.

He might have phoned Swaziland from Hong Kong. Or he might even be home, and if he discovers I'm not there and that I'm not at Cathy's he'll be worried. What's going to happen about your business, if you stay here with me? I've been worrying about that.'

'I can handle things from here. You have a phone, don't you?' Hugo took her hand and touched her fingers with his lips. 'I'll be brief with you,' he said. 'I want to stay with you.'

'You're only saying that because you've been drinking,' she said, feeling on dangerous ground now. Her heartbeat quickened. When he began to stroke her jawline, beneath her hair, her green eyes did not leave his face. Sometimes, she thought, his face could be so hard. After a moment he sat back, his dark blue eyes, half-closed, surveying her intensely, and she realised the desire he was feeling for her and the undeniable hunger. That's all he thinks of, she told herself bitterly, but when he took her into his arms she felt bitterness slipping away from her and responded eagerly. A wildness rose up in her and fought off all thinking from her mind. He had undone the tortoiseshell clasp in her hair and it fell about her face and he moved it away impatiently, so that he could kiss her lips. His hands moved in exploration of her body and his weight on her became heavy.

'I have been drinking, yes,' he said, against her mouth, 'but believe me, my physical reactions are still good enough for me to want to make love to you.'

For a moment the pain was so severe that she

thought he must have torn the stitches from her leg, and she cried out, 'Hugo—my leg! *Get off me!*'

When he drew away from her he sounded more than usually cold when he said, 'I'm sorry. I'm being unreasonable. Sleep in peace, Tirza.'

CHAPTER SEVEN

AFTER two days and nights of dragging pain Tirza was beginning to feel drained and helpless. She could not walk without difficulty and her head ached. To add to this, she lived in fear that it would be discovered that Delphina's snarling, saliva-dripping mongrel was rabid. Certainly, as she had looked into those curious yellow eyes she had been aware of canine madness. Waiting for the verdict stretched before her, like a death sentence.

Hugo spent most of his time in the pool and she would follow him outdoors to watch him moodily from a chaise-longue. It was strange the effect he had on her. There was always an intense awareness of herself and because she longed for him to touch and comfort her, she felt cheated.

In a garden smelling of flowers and wild tobacco plants, her father's gardeners kept everything in perfect order. Sun-umbrellas, patterned in massed poppies, white daisies, pink carnations, yellow lilies and cerise cosmos splashed against a background of wrapping-paper brown were dotted here and there. It was all so typical of Douglas Harper's luxuriously appointed homes. Everything was larger than life—even the sun-umbrellas. It was just another perfect house in a perfect garden in perfect sheep farming conditions, Tirza thought with some bitterness, waiting for an owner who seldom came

... like the chalet in the Berg and the house that clung to the dunes at Plettenberg Bay. Wild pink roses clung to white pillars and to cope with the heat there were tall grasses, trees and flowering shrubs and that oval, glittering expanse of blue water, filtered and invigorating. The roof tiles of the house, although giving the appearance of blue slate, were of asbestos. This, together with fibreglass insulation, kept out a great deal of summer heat.

They could have been in a world that time had forgotten. In fact, it was a private oasis, brought to life by people who were being paid, and paid well, by Douglas Harper. An oasis in the semidesert like Karroo which could be harsh, both in winter and in summer, and yet so strangely beautiful and exciting.

Delphina made rusks and *koeksusters* and *melkterts*, the recipes of which had been handed down from generation to generation.

In different circumstances, Tirza thought wistfully, it could have been wonderful. She gazed at Hugo, who was in the pool now, and then she closed her eyes in frustration, her fingers going to the back of her knee which was still paining her. Her slim shoulders slumped in an angry impotent gesture. How she would love to be there in that sparkling water instead of just sitting here in her bikini! The tiny bra of the bikini left most of her bosom uncovered and her small breasts had taken on a coppery colour, and even her buttocks blended in with her tanned legs.

While she had been confined to her bed, nursing

her pain, Hugo had gone into the nearest Karroo town and after he had driven away the silence of the Karroo had engulfed her, as she waited for him to return. When he did, it was with food and fruit and liquor, and the kind of mineral waters to go with it. He had brought back wines to have with their meals and a pile of glossy magazines.

Eventually the day arrived when Gerry Strauss came to remove the stitches. After he had gone Hugo said, 'Tomorrow I'll take you out—to break the boredom.'

Tirza glanced at him resentfully. So he had been bored, she thought.

In a stiff little voice she asked, 'Where will you take me?'

'Oh,' he shrugged, 'maybe we'll drive into town and look around . . . buy . . .'

'Buy—what?' She struggled to hide her depression.

'Anything that happens to take our fancy. While I was there the other day I saw an interesting little antique shop.'

'That would be nice,' she murmured, and then, to keep him talking, she went on, 'Tell me about your house, Hugo.'

'The house in Swaziland? It's just a cottage, really. Nothing spectacular—quite attractive, though. There's a garden with a filtered pool.'

'I meant the one in Cape Town, actually.'

'Oh.' He sounded surprised. 'It used to be a labourer's cottage. It's set on a long, sloping plot at the foot of Table Mountain.'

'That sounds beautiful.'

'It's nothing like your father's mansion in Cape Town, or the one here. Strangely enough, though, it's the last remaining portion of *a farm* called White Tablecloth Farm, so named, of course, because of the cloud formation that spreads itself over the mountain. It had one big drawback, however, and that is why I was able to buy it, at my price. Because of a steep incline, it had no roadway to the street. Anyway, I went ahead and bought it, simply because the beauty of the plot outweighed all disadvantages, so far as I was concerned. I bought it, and the cottage on it, and I've created a very private world for myself. Hiring somebody to bulldoze the property and construct a road, at a staggering fee, nearly broke me, at the time, but it was well worth it.'

Tirza was interested. 'How old is the house?'

'The cottage is a hundred years old. The costs of alterations and additions and swimming-pool were high, and as I mentioned, nearly broke me, because at the time of all this there still was no roadway and everything had to be carried there by hand.'

'You're nearly as bad as my father,' she said, after a moment.

'What's that supposed to mean?'

'With your properties, I mean.'

Hugo laughed at that, and looked about the flower-scented and landscaped garden. 'Nobody could be as bad as your father,' he said sarcastically. 'As I see it, Douglas Harper and his beautiful daughter don't lack for much.' His blue eyes went over the robe she was wearing, which looked simple enough to be wildly expensive. 'I've noticed all the clothes, of course—laid on, just as they are, no doubt, laid on for you to use at whichever house you happen to be visiting.'

'Sometimes I really detest you,' she said swiftly. 'Do you know that?'

'I'm just being realistic,' Hugo replied. 'You're spoilt.' Although his eyes were mocking, there was a hard look to go along with the mockery.

Tirza was seething now. 'Thank you. And a cheat too, I suppose—to add to your list.'

'Well,' he shrugged, 'it's true, isn't it?'

After a moment she said, 'Well, the stitches are out and I'm able to get around. As far as I'm concerned you can leave here whenever you like. I'll make my own arrangements about getting back to Cape Town. In any case, I'd intended asking Gerry whether I could go back and wait there for the verdict. In fact, I think my father would prefer that . . . when he gets to hear about the dog-bite. I still haven't been able to get him on the phone, though.'

'When I leave here,' Hugo sounded annoyed, 'you'll be with me. What do you take me for?'

He had been swimming, as usual, and Tirza had been sitting watching him in her bikini when Gerry had arrived to remove the stitches. Directly Gerry had done this she had slipped into her robe.

By now, the first star of the evening had begun to glitter and the scent of petunias was heavy. In the distance, and past the bronze lions that crouched beside the water, the Karroo koppies looked dusky-pink. The star was reflected in the water which was still moving about after Hugo's swim. The filter had cut off, for the night, and would start again in the morning.

He came towards her. 'Let me help you inside.'

Her expression, when she answered him, was wooden. 'I can manage myself, thank you. The stitches are out, don't forget.'

'I hadn't forgotten,' he said, suddenly enclosing her possessively with his arms. 'The prerogative of a man is to command and of a woman to obey.' Except for his swimming trunks, he was naked, and his tan looked deeper in this light. In fact, it even appeared like theatrical make-up and when she looked into his eyes she might have been looking into dark blue grottoes. She had grown to learn that the colour of his eyes depended on his mood.

His eyes were on her face now, and she thought he was going to kiss her, then the expression in them changed to almost boredom.

'Don't fight me, Tirza,' he said. 'I don't like it.' He dropped his arms to his side.

She stood looking at him and combed her hair back from her forehead with her fingers, then twisted it into a knot, high on her head, looking in her loose-hanging white robe like a Greek goddess.

She made no protest, however, when Hugo took her fingers in his own and began to walk towards the house, and when they were in the Italian-tiled hall he said, 'I'm going to shower. Afterwards, I'll join you for a drink. Personally, I find all this as tiresome as you do yourself. But I want to make it quite clear—we'll travel to Cape Town together. What you do after that, about coming here to start your own weaving industry, doesn't concern me in the least. My concern is to get you back to Cape Town, where you can be watched by your family doctor.'

Fear leapt into her eyes. 'Do you know something?' she asked, in a strangled voice.

'What are you talking about?'

'Was the dog—rabid?'

He must have realised how deeply worried she was, and the stern lines on his face relaxed. 'I don't believe the dog was rabid,' he told her, in a softer tone of voice. 'It makes sense, though, doesn't it ... after all you've been through? For one thing, you've lost weight. A doctor might well prescribe a tonic.'

'Yes, I suppose you're right,' she agreed.

After she left him, she took a bath and was thankful to be able to soak her leg, and she lay back in the hot, perfume-drenched water, stretching her body and enjoying the heat which was sensuous, somehow, and made her forget about the threat of rabies.

Afterwards, regardless of what Hugo would think, she went to her wardrobe and took out a cinnamon-coloured skirt, which had tiny apricot coloured roses and green leaves splashed across it and a darker cinnamon top. She applied eyeshadow and mascara, coloured her lips and added a touch of gloss.

Hugo was in the lounge when she got there, and his blue eyes went lazily over her. Her high-heeled sandals were all straps and, because she was not wearing stockings, she could feel the thickly-piled carpeting against her bare flesh, and the feel of it accentuated her awareness of herself—that and the sheer maleness of Hugo. Because of the heat, he had left his silk shirt unbuttoned and the cuffs were turned back. His trousers were well cut and emphasised his hard flat stomach.

'Ah,' he turned, 'here comes Charlie, is it?'

'Is there a law against wearing Charlie?' she asked.

'No, not at all, especially when that tantalising fragrance is followed by a girl as beautiful as a tawny cat, with green eyes, and who knows how to live with complete abandon.'

'That's absolute nonsense!' she spoke impatiently. 'How can you say that? You hardly know me. I don't live with complete abandon.'

'I know enough about you, by now, to put two and two together,' he sounded amused.

A feeling of jealousy swept over. 'Does Paige use Charlie?'

'Don't try to trap me into talking about another woman when I happen to be with you. Why bring Paige into the picture? I wasn't thinking about Paige, as it so happens,' he answered, at his most crisp.

'Perhaps I should tell you about her,' said Tirza. 'I think it's about time you did know about Paige Mobray, and her mother. Paige, you see, very nearly became my stepsister, or whatever you like to call it. In other words, Mr Harrington, this mansion was prepared for Cathy Mobray who was about to marry my father. For reasons known only to herself, however, she changed her mind. Perhaps it was the lady's love of gambling. Who knows?

She would have been far too cut off from the casino, that's for sure. I was only told about this just before I left for Swaziland. In fact, that's how I came to stay with Cathy. It was a stipulation my father made when I left on my buying trip. Why don't you laugh at that? But yes, I was on a buying trip to Swaziland. This buying trip was to be combined with modelling for the Swazi Signature. My father didn't know about that, of course.'

'Of course modelling for Swazi Signature had its uses,' his voice was hard. 'I mean—it was, after all, your way of finding out more about the industry. It was, as you yourself have a habit of saying, "another iron in the fire". Right?'

The anger in her was wrestling to be released. Usually, Hugo mixed their drinks before dinner, but she went towards the cabinet now.

'Why stoop to Cathy's level?' His voice was hard. 'Why tell me? I'm not interested.'

'Talk about *stooping*,' she swung round, '*you* seemed to enjoy listening to her gossip, didn't you? That's how you learned all about me, who I really was, and all about my snide little plans. *I* didn't have to tell you anything. In fact, you didn't even give me a chance. Let me tell you something— there's a lot about me you still don't know . . . like the times I'm left alone at the house in Bishopscourt, while my father is on an extensive business trip.' She turned away and fumbled with glasses. 'Sometimes whole weeks go by and I never see him. My father's mansions are like expensive waiting rooms. Oh, he phones home, of course— long distance calls aren't something my father thinks about twice.' She was quiet for a moment, her fingers busy. '*You* are very like him, actually.' Her voice was soft and bitter.

Again his impatience flared. 'So you've said before. I still find that hard to believe, however.'

'It's true.' Her voice rose a little. 'You're both so ambitious. Like you, he's often—abrupt. He seldom confides in me. In a roundabout way I heard about this sheep farm he was buying and the hotel which was being converted into this mansion farmhouse. Isn't that wild? I found myself wondering at the time what he wanted a sheep farm for.' She swung around, a glass in each hand, spilling a little of the liquid from both glasses. 'A sheep farm? Angora goats? Douglas Harper?' Suddenly she laughed.

'And, to get even with him, you're putting the farm to better use. Anything Papa can do I can do better. You don't appear to lack ambition yourself,' observed Hugo.

'I only got to know about this place when he brought me here with his architect,' she went on. 'This house used to be the Merino Hotel. It was a white elephant, actually, believe it or not. It was too cut off for the average holidaymaker. The original farmhouse was converted for Gerry and his wife. Even while we were here on this particular visit, Cathy's name was never mentioned. But at the end of everything Cathy backed out. I mean, what would she have done without a gambling casino practically on her doorstep?'

'Go on,' said Hugo, 'don't stop. There's no one in the room, except me.'

When she made to set the glasses down again he came towards her. 'Here,' he said, 'you're spilling the damned stuff.'

'What does it matter?' she cried. 'What can it possibly matter to you, you uncaring devil!' Before she realised what she was doing she hurled one of the glasses in the direction of the hall where it splintered on the beautiful tiled floor.

'If you want an audience for your tantrums,' Hugo snapped, 'count me out. Being in this house with you, Tirza, is beginning to get on my nerves!'

Pushing the tears back up her cheeks with her fingertips, she told him, 'You're free to leave, whenever you wish. Why stay on?'

'Look,' he said, in a different voice, 'I know you've been in pain and that you've been worried— and don't think I haven't thought about this. I have. And that makes it all the more inexcusable that I should have lashed out at you a moment ago.'

When she made no reply he said, 'Tirza?'

She felt like breaking. 'It's okay. Okay?' She took a long calming breath. 'Just get out of my life! Had it ever struck you that I might just be sick of you too?'

The two chandeliers were burning, but dimmed, and the lounge with its pale apricot walls, white fireplace, black beams and gold curtains seemed to be wrapped in glowing gold-warmed hues. There were blue hydrangeas on the low table that stood between the floral sofas flanking the fireplace—and there was a smashed cut-glass goblet on the Italian-tiled floor in the hall.

There seemed to be no colour in Tirza's face now and it was like the face of a bronze statue.

'I shouldn't have said all that,' her voice was toneless. 'You see, I love my father.'

There was between them an almost tangible awareness and she watched him as he put his glass down, aware of his blue eyes on her all the time, and she was shocked at the expression in them, behind their thick black growth of lashes. When he reached for her she did not resist. Nor did she resist when his mouth came down on her own. He drew her very close, moulding her body against his own, and his lips became more demanding, and she knew, very well, that the primitive element to kissing her was merely the male arrogance in him stating that he intended to possess her before they left this house. She was rocked to her being and every reasoning power she believed she had was brushed aside.

'Marry me,' he said, holding her away from him.

'Why?' Her heart was thudding. 'Why, Hugo?' Her eyes held his.

'Well,' he went on looking at her, 'with all the irons in the fire, we could form quite a team. We'd combine businesses. Together, we should be a great success.'

'It—it might just surprise you if I say yes,' she whispered. 'You know how to hurt me, don't you? You would even go so far as to marry me—just to hurt me—to punish me for being Tirza *Theron* Harper. You're ruthless, you're conceited and you're . . .'

He cut in, 'Nevertheless, think about it.'

'Yes. Make no mistake—I'll think about it. I *am*. You despise my father's money, and all it can buy, and yet you wouldn't mind a share in it. It's perfectly plain now. I think you're despicable! But yet, I will think about it. You see, it might just suit *me* to marry you. I guess you hadn't thought about that one, had you?'

At that moment Delphina came to announce that dinner would be served in the indoor patio and, confused, Tirza thanked her, for she had been aware of Delphina's shocked eyes going to the broken glass and spilled liquid on the tiled floor in the hall, as she had stepped around them.

The indoor patio was furnished in cane, upholstered in bronze, cinnamon, black and white fabric, and Douglas Harper had arranged for a television set to be installed here. On the outside there were ginger and white striped canvas awnings at the windows, which were set in arches. Everywhere in this house there was this extravagant and lavish touch. They ate dinner at a glass-topped cane table, set with crystal goblets and gleaming silver. The cane chairs were high-backed and intricately scrolled. After dinner Hugo turned on the television and, feeling tense beyond words, Tirza stood up. 'I'm going for a swim,' she said.

'That scar might be vulnerable to infection,' he hardly gave her a glance. Obviously he had forgotten that only a short while ago he had proposed to her, she thought bitterly.

'It seemed all right when Gerry took the stitches out,' she said.

With considerable impatience he glanced away from the television set and said, 'Can't you hang out for a couple of days? Why argue about something that makes sense?'

'I don't think it makes sense. In fact, nothing makes sense to me any more,' she stormed at him, and then rushed from the room. All that made sense, she thought wildly, was that she was willing to take the risk of marrying Hugo, willing to throw prudence to the winds.

He was in the pool when she got there and she saw him look up at her and guessed, correctly, that he was angry with her. 'Don't be a fool,' he said. 'Keep out of the water, for a day or two.'

'I am a fool,' she said. 'If I wasn't, I wouldn't be here with you now.'

'That happens to be beside the point.' She heard the anger in his voice. 'Let's not make a drama about this, Tirza.'

'If I want to swim, I'll swim,' she replied with childish bravado, as she slipped out of the jacket she was wearing over her bikini and tossed it over a chair. The enormous red poppies, yellow sunflowers and green leaves in the material looked almost real. For a moment she looked sleek and beautiful in the moonlight and the light coming from the garden lamps and underwater light of the pool, before she did a neat dive and vanished in a swirl of translucent turquoise-blue water. When she surface she discovered that she had come up near him.

'You always seem to go through life with an imperious indifference to possible danger,' he said.

'I don't think I do. Often I'm only too aware of danger—only half the time, there's never anybody around to share those fears with me. Right now, I'm aware of danger, as it so happens.' She began a slow crawl away from him and she was very flat on the water and her style was good.

'Very good,' he called out. 'If that was meant to impress me—I'm very impressed. But then you've been perfectly coached, quite obviously. You are talented and beautiful—enough to excite any man, even when the man happens to be married. No doubt, he was one of many.'

Suddenly she hoisted herself from the water and stood looking down at him before she picked up a towel and began to dry herself. Silver drops of water that clung to her smooth tan were easily seen in the softly glowing light which suffused this part of the garden. The Karroo night was silent and the air was perfumed with night-scented tobacco plants, their pale flowers gleaming beneath the stars.

'Oh yes, I've had a string of affairs. I thrive on variety,' she told him.

'I believe that,' he flung back at her. 'I can quite believe that the intimacies you've shared with me—plus some more—have been shared with countless other men.'

'It makes no difference to me what you believe. Go ahead, feel free—but if you want to marry me, you'll just have to accept me the way I am, for I'll accept your proposal, if it's still open, of marriage.' She laughed carelessly, but her heart was racing. 'Getting married for business reasons has its advantages—even *I* can see that.'

Tirza had slicked her wet hair right back from her face and it was easy to see that thin white line where her tan ended and her hair began. Tiny circles of gold glinted in each ear. A full orchestra of crickets filled the otherwise quiet air.

When Hugo had hoisted himself from the water he strode to where she was standing, and she caught her breath as he grabbed her wrist between his fingers. 'Do you ever stop to think?' he asked.

'Yes, I do. I think all the time, believe me. You and I do have much in common. You've called me ambitious and nobody can deny that *you* are ambitious. And then there's my father's money, isn't there? It will come in very useful. I mean, you did say that bulldozing your place in Cape Town very nearly broke you, didn't you?'

'I'll advise you not to judge me on your imagination, over which, I might add, you appear to have no control. Money has never been my undoing, Tirza.' His grip on her wrist tightened. 'Just put that on record. What's more—especially when that money doesn't happen to be my own. If you marry me, Miss Harper, you won't exactly be marrying a poor man.'

'There is no if about it. I am willing to marry you. But, while we are having this discussion, isn't this just what you have done? You've judged me on your imagination.' She glanced down at her wrist. 'Will you let go of me, please? You have a cold, calculating character.'

'To match your own, in fact,' he answered. When he kissed her she had the weakening but exciting feeling that she and Hugo were both caught in a slowing down of time, as if they could go on kissing like this, for long, long minutes, with no particular urgency until the moment when they both realised that only complete surrender on her part could assuage the hunger that was mounting in both of them. Tirza realised that his power over her was such that she would deny him nothing. To her humiliation, however, he released her suddenly and reached for her jacket and draped it about her shoulders.

'I suggest you go and change,' he told her, 'and I suggest, also, that you put an antiseptic of some sort on that scar, which still looks inflamed enough to give rise to trouble. Tomorrow we'll go into town and make arrangements to be married by special licence. So that rules out all those charmingly engraved invitations, St Joseph and arum lilies and a veil.'

'So our marriage is still on?' Her breath was coming fast and she moistened her lips with the tip of her tongue. 'You still intend to go through with this farce?'

'Yes, of course. Marrying you will have its advantages and so that makes two of us.' Hugo's eyes went over her. 'There are worse things than marrying for business reasons.'

In the morning Tirza was up early and devoted time going through the clothes hanging in cupboards and folded in drawers—clothes she had almost forgotten about ... abandoned ... It seemed incredible that this was her way of life. What was there here, forgotten about until this

moment, for her to wear on her unbelievable
wedding day— for she was drifting into it without
any thought of the future.

At the time of visiting the farm with her father
and the Winters, she remembered she had been
madly attracted to vivid, handcrafted clothes made
in loosely-woven cotton fabrics worn by the
Shangaan, Venda and Lobedu tribes. She took out
a scarlet Shangaan caftan, which had widely-
spaced stripes at intervals all the way up, in cream,
brown and black. Well, she mused, that was out.
A blushing bride would hardly sweep the pavements of a Karroo town with it, on her wedding
day. A label inside the neckline stated that the garment was from the Kuziwe Range, created by
Dolores Perkins. Nothing but the best for Miss
Tirza Theron Harper, she thought bitterly.

The next garment was off the shoulder and
therefore not suitable. It was beautiful, though,
with gathered long sleeves and skirt created out of
Shangaan fabric which had wine-red and slate-blue
bands. And then came the Swazi Mahia wrapover
which, because of its name alone, should be appropriate. The brown Mahia print was patterned
with cream loops and squares, and Tirza re-
collected there had been beads to go with it. Cream
coloured ostrich beads, and the necklace was so
long that she used to twist it three times round her
neck, and even then the strands fell to beyond her
waist. The Mahia wrapover it would be. After all,
she knew from experience that the colour did things
for her tan, but after she and Hugo were married
and got back to the farm, she would change for

dinner, she thought. She would get Delphina to prepare Karroo partridge that night and she would invite Gerry round for drinks, although he had no idea of the drama which was being played out in this house, right at this moment. After searching around for the bronzy-brown high-heeled sandals to go with the dress, she put them all to one side and went down to the lounge, where she poured herself a sherry. Her hands were shaking and she went to one of the huge windows.

Hugo was in the pool, and he was the man she was going to marry. He was also the man who had received a telephone call from Paige Mobray that very morning . . . and she watched him moodily. It was a staggering thought that, if she had not been bitten by Delphina's dog, this would never have happened to her. Hugo would have gone back to his house in Cape Town and possibly she would have travelled back with him, where they would have parted.

Glass in hand, she went out to the pool. Magenta bougainvillaea, in white tubs, was reflected in the filtered pool and the colour seemed to be dancing around Hugo in the water. Directly he looked up at her Tirza saw his eyes go to her glass and, because it was such a hostile glance, she said flippantly, 'You know, I was just thinking—you might well end up with a mad wife. If Delphina's dog was rabid, you know. Do people who've been bitten by a rabid dog go mad, or what? I've never known.' She took a sip of her sherry, as fear washed over her and she realised how tense she had been with the thought of rabies never very far from her mind.

'Cut that out,' he snapped. 'Okay?' She watched him as he got out of the water. 'What's the drink in aid of?' he asked, while he reached for his towel. 'At this time of day?'

'I've been busy,' she told him. 'I've been choosing my wedding outfit for the civil ceremony.'

'And that warrants drinking sherry at this time of the day?'

'How did you know it was sherry?' She took another sip.

'I can smell it's sherry.' He sounded impatient.

'I'm unsettled,' she went on. 'Everything seems so—so unbelievable and unreal.' Her troubled green eyes went over his face and she longed for him to take her into his arms, wet as he was, and to hold her very close and to tell her that he loved her. When he remained silent she said, 'Despite Women's Lib, you know, brides still want to appear fragile and lovely.' Her voice was superficial and carelessly frivolous.

'There's nothing fragile about you,' he said cruelly. 'If there were, you wouldn't be marrying me.'

'Don't you want to marry me?' she taunted.

'Try to figure it out for yourself,' he snapped, 'but go on, I'm interested—being the future groom and all that.'

'Well, the outfit I've chosen, and I hope you'll approve, happens to be of Swazi origin, which I think is very appropriate.'

She watched him moodily as he went on drying himself. 'You make a drama out of everything.'

His dark blue eyes came back to her. 'What difference does it make what you wear? Maybe you can see some humour in this, Tirza, but I'm afraid it escapes me. However, in the circumstances, I suppose it's just as well you left it behind, along with all the other items of clothing.'

The dry air was faintly perfumed and Tirza thought it must be drifting in from those stunted Karroo bushes and she knew that she would always remember it.

'When you're ready, we can drive into town and arrange a special licence,' he told her.

'Do you mean—today?' She looked at him with wide eyes.

'Yes. Unless you've changed your mind?'

'No, I haven't.' She turned away from him, afraid for him to see what was written in her eyes.

In the late afternoon they drove into the small town. Hugo was wearing a casual oatmeal suit which she had not seen before and which emphasised his hard, lean body. He was, she thought, feeling the need to breathe deeper, completely and utterly male, and she was going to be his wife.

The Karroo today was majestic, vast and endless. Those silent, brooding and flat-topped koppies looked almost amethyst in the distance. At close range they became khaki-green, but still exciting, for the very reason that they were so barren. The vast arid plains were dotted with remote farmhouses, simple of architecture but orientated towards the extreme heat. The windmills were motionless, although there was a small, pulsing breeze to arouse the senses.

Hugo seemed preoccupied and disinclined to talk, so she stared out of the open window. This was, she thought, the land of merino sheep. The wool-store, in fact, of the country, and her father owned a part of it and, because of the Swazi Signature Weaving Industry in Swaziland, Hugo also had an interest in it. So much so, in fact, that he had even proposed this reckless marriage merely because it suited him.

He broke into her thoughts and, surprised, she turned to look at him. 'I didn't hear what you said. I'm sorry, I was miles away . . .'

'I said, did you know that many famous astronomers visit the Karroo to study the stars?' He turned to look at her.

'No, I didn't. It's strange—I was also thinking of the Karroo.' For some unknown reason she experienced a thrill.

Sunlight gilded everything in the small Karroo town—even the fine particles of dust which floated about in the office where they made the necessary arrangements to be married in three days' time.

'Well,' said Hugo when they were outside the building, 'our union will be legalised at the end of the week.' He surprised her by bending his head to kiss her lightly on the lips. 'And then I'll be boss—and just remember that!' He smiled faintly.

'You always *have* been boss,' she replied.

Later he took her to the little antique shop he had told her about. It was a ramshackle building, and a dog was sleeping on a mat, next to the door, and Tirza found herself tensing as she stared down at it, afraid to pass.

'It's all right.' Hugo took her hand, and at that moment the dog yawned. The yawn sounded like protesting brakes and they both laughed; Hugo looked suddenly very boyish, and Tirza found herself biting her lip, to keep back the tears that threatened to engulf her.

Still holding hands, they went inside the shop, which came as a surprise. There were copper utensils, dressers, butter-churns and many other items, characteristic of the old Cape. A love-seat was inlaid with intricately patterned ivory and stood next to a pair of French cupboards, also inlaid with ivory and many kinds of wood.

Hugo bought her four crudely painted bowl-like cups, with matching saucers, which had been found beneath the floorboards of an old house. The house was believed to be about two hundred years old. Crude as they were, there was a strange beauty about the cups and saucers.

In the car, going back to the farm, Tirza knew that Hugo was glancing at her from time to time, and smiling too, it seemed. 'Have you enjoyed yourself?' he asked.

'Yes.' She bit her lip. 'I have, actually. It was wonderful to get away from the farm for a while.'

'Was that the only reason?'

'Well, no.' She felt her cheeks flushing. 'You—you bought me a present, didn't you? I love them.'

He parked the car beneath the large pillared portico and when they went inside the last rays of the sun were slanting across the shaggy golden carpet and highlighting the Persian rugs which had been placed on it. A gentle sunset breeze brought the smell of the Karroo flowers right into the house.

The telephone rang and when Tirza answered it, Gerry Strauss said, 'Hi, Tirza. How's tricks?'

'Fine, thank you.'

'How's the leg?'

'Oh, fine. Is Zelma back yet, Gerry?'

'No,' he answered. 'Her mother wants her to stay on there for a few more days.'

'I see. Well, why don't you come over for a drink?'

'When?' He sounded interested.

'Now.' Tirza laughed lightly.

Going back into the lounge, she said, 'That was Gerry Strauss. I've invited him over for a drink. Zelma isn't back yet.'

'Suits me,' said Hugo.

In her room, she struggled a long time with her hair until, satisfied, she turned away from the mirror. She had scooped it severely on to the top of her head into a coiled topknot and then she had wound a wide bracelet of colourful African bead-work around it. She fastened another bracelet around her upper arm. Her shoulders and midriff were bare and golden-brown, for she had changed into the long, flounced Shangaan skirt and halter top. The colours of the wide horizontal stripes matched the bracelets—dark blue, light blue, white, burnt-orange and a darker red. She had taken great trouble with her appearance and she looked beau-tiful and radiant.

Her life, she found herself thinking, was becom-ing like something out of a motion picture. This magnificent farmhouse in the semi-desert Karroo, glamorous clothes which had just been waiting for her to come back and enjoy them . . . but then *her* life, although a lonely one, had this fictitious touch to it—simply because she happened to be Douglas Harper's daughter.

Gerry arrived soon after she had entered the lounge where, because it had turned unexpectedly cool, there was a fire crackling in the white fireplace. After all the heat of the past few days it was, somehow, exhilarating to feel the new chill in the air.

Looking around, Gerry surprised her by saying, 'This looks like some kind of celebration. Is it?' His eyes went back to Tirza.

After a moment Hugo said, 'We're to be married. We went into town this afternoon to arrange things.' He had changed into casual dark trousers and a dark silk shirt. A gold medallion glistened through the dark curly hairs on his tanned chest and, looking at him, Tirza suppressed a shiver.

'I thought there was something in the air,' Gerry said cheerfully, 'right from the moment I saw you both. I didn't see a ring on your finger, though.' He looked at Tirza again. 'It was the first thing I looked for, as a matter of fact. Well, here's luck. I hope you'll both be very happy.'

'We'll be spending a lot of our time here,' Tirza told him, not looking in Hugo's direction. 'You see, we're putting this farm to further use. There's going to be a thriving weaving industry here, Gerry.'

'Well, what do you know?' Gerry sounded pleased.

After he had gone the room seemed very still, and Tirza realised, suddenly, that she felt a little intoxicated and remembered that, having skipped breakfast and lunch, she had hardly eaten a thing all day.

Over his glass, now, Hugo was watching her and then he said softly, 'You're very beautiful.'

'You once said that my mouth was too wide,' she replied, with an attempt at carelessness, 'but thank you anyway. You don't have to say these things, though.'

'Don't I?' His eyes went over her.

'No.'

'You must know by now,' he went on, 'that I want to make love to you?'

'I do know it,' she murmured, and lowered her eyelashes.

She watched him as he placed his glass on the low table. He came over to where she was sitting and went down on the floor beside her. She put her hands, with their beautiful oval nails, on either side of his face. 'It's not the same as—loving—is it?' she said.

'It will have to do.' Suddenly his voice was abrupt. Then he put his fingers against her cheek and began a slow, sensual exploration of her shoulder, going to the back of her neck and then up to the topknot, which he tried to undo.

'Don't,' she said, unable to bear the tension. 'You're always trying to undo my hair, when I put it up.'

Hugo began fumbling with the buttons of her halter top.

'Why did you have to choose to wear something that has the kind of tiny buttons which defy clumsy male fingers?' he asked, his voice soft and thick.

'I don't want you to do that,' she told him, pressing her fingers against his shoulders.

'Why not?'

'I'm not in the mood.' After a moment she said, 'Why is it that a girl subconsciously observes her father as the typical husband and she often ends up marrying a man very much like her father? It certainly seems as if I might be going to do just that, unfortunately.'

'Generalisation is the hallmark of a complete fool,' he answered. 'On what do you base the conclusion that I'm like your father?' He stood up and looked down at her. 'If he's the type of man who becomes impatient with stupidity and is accustomed to issuing orders which he expects to be instantly and intelligently carried out, then I suppose I am like him.'

'You are,' she replied. 'Into the bargain, you have two houses—so does he. Right?'

'One is nothing more than a cottage—the one in Swaziland. I told you about it. Once we're married and whenever we feel the pressures of city life closing in on us, or when the demands of the weaving industries, here or in Swaziland, become too much for us, we can flee to it.' His voice was sarcastic. 'The other, in Cape Town, would hardly fit into the Douglas Harper category.'

'You also appear to go away on business trips,'

she went on. 'And what's more, you even *look* like him.'

'Look like him?' His voice took on a tone of disbelief. 'As usual, you are exaggerating.'

'You do look like him. I often find myself thinking about this. You could be his son. He's slightly shorter than you are—and heavier, of course.'

There was a pause and then he said, 'You sound as though you don't like your father. But remember, no father is perfect, but I should say, all fathers are precious.'

'I like him very much.' Her voice rose. 'More than that, I happen to love him. My father is a marvellous person. He's a genius in the world of high finance, but that doesn't mean he doesn't care for music, theatre, painting and the decorative arts. He does. It's just that he's never there when I need him.'

'When we get back to Cape Town and you make the discovery that I don't, in fact, look like your father and that I'm nothing like him and that I happen to be the man you've married, you'll have some readjusting to do.' There was a wry twist to his mouth. 'In fact, before we leave this house you'll have some readjusting to do. You will also have to adjust to the fact that there will be no other man in your life. I refer, of course, to the character I saw you with on the Eastern Boulevard, Tirza, because I realise that he's at the back of things. I doubt if you'd have got round to the scheme of a weaving industry if it hadn't been for your broken heart.'

'There's no need for you to bring that up,' she

told him. 'I'm over the hump so far as he's concerned.

'Were there others?' he asked. 'Others who know about the peacock in the jungle dream?'

'What you mean is, have I slept with men? Have I had affairs? Well, yes, I've had strings of affairs. My father's mansion bustled with my lovers. Is that what you crave to hear? In any case, how can it concern you? You don't love me. Our marriage will be in the sole interest of business—yours and mine. Into the bargain, there were those costs of alterations and additions to your house and the site, and the cost of building a swimming-pool. Well, marrying me will have its compensations. Just put the idea of my lovers from your mind.'

'You'll be my wife, that's how it concerns me,' Hugo snapped. 'The way in which you chose to lead your life before you met me is your own business. After we're married, however, it will become my business.'

'After we're married it will not mean you'll get preferential treatment. I doubt if *I*'ll get it, judging on the way Paige Mobray phones this house.'

When he came back over to her and caught her wrist and pulled her up to him she bit her lip. 'This may help to restore your memory—that I've asked you to marry me—and that just happens to mean united in wedlock—and that you've accepted. Therefore, when we're married, you will not see this character in Cape Town, or any man, for that matter.' His expression chilled her. 'For what it's worth, this marriage is going to work. Understand?'

It was strange the effect he had on her, she

thought, as she waited for his kiss which was, she knew, merely a seal of his possession of her. His lips were hard and demanding and she felt her mounting excitement and her immediate response. A silky warmth spread over her body, leaving her peculiarly weak and dizzy, and she pressed harder against him in a mist of desire, parting her lips, wanting to shock him and hurt herself, she supposed dreamily, for she wanted Hugo on any terms. Perhaps it would work, perhaps he would grow to love her . . .

His arms tightened around her and she longed for him to pick her up and carry her to her room. Instead, however, he released her abruptly. 'Just you remember that,' he told her. 'You don't know me, Tirza. The past is gone. It's the present I'm concerned about. I'm not in the mood to be irritated, goaded or shocked. I'd say it was about high time you came to your senses over this. You seem to be missing the point. You're going to marry me and you're going to be married to me for a long time.'

When he left her, Tirza remained standing where she was for several minutes. She realised that, as Hugo had been lashing out at her, her teeth had plunged themselves into her lower lip. Suddenly she sat down on the carpet and drew her knees up and encircled them with her arms, and she was still sitting in this position when she heard a car approaching the portico outside and, believing it to be her father, she stood up swiftly, her hands going to her cheeks.

When she went into the hall she saw Nigel

Wright getting out of his car and her breath caught and died in her throat. Coming towards her, he said easily, 'Who were you expecting?'

'My father, as it happens.' Her eyes were riveted on his face. 'What are you doing here? Who told you I was here?'

'Mrs Meeker. Who else?' He laughed softly.

Tirza stood staring at him with her face appalled. 'You have a nerve, Nigel, coming here!'

'I don't think so. Look, Tirza, Lorna might agree to divorce me. It's on the cards.'

'She *might* agree?' There was contempt in her voice. 'Lorna might agree to divorce you? Oh, get out of my sight! I don't want you here.'

'We had a kingsize row,' he went on. 'She packed her bags and left. I've been on the razzle ever since, as a matter of fact. Geez . . .' he laughed and ran his fingers through his hair. 'I've been looking for you.' He stepped forward and placed his hands on her shoulders.

'Get away from me!' she hissed, moving away.

'Come on, Tirza.'

'Go away, damn you! I don't want you here, especially now.'

'Why else did you clear off to the Karroo?' he asked. 'Mrs Meeker told me you were here. That, so far as I was concerned, summed it up in a nutshell—you were trying to get over me. Well now, there's no need to, I tell you.' Before she could stop him he had his arms about her and his lips were upon her own, and she could smell that he had been drinking.

'I appear to have chosen an inconvenient time to

arrive back from a stroll in the garden.' Hugo's voice cut into the scene.

'Well, well, well, you've been busy, I see.' Nigel's arms dropped to his sides. 'It didn't take you long, girl.' Turning to Hugo, he said, 'By now, you'll know all about Tirza's peacock in the jungle dream—and the screaming that goes along with it.'

'Hugo,' Tirza's voice rose, 'don't listen to him, please! He only knows about the dream because I *told* him about it. You've got to believe me. It's the truth! You had a nerve coming here, Nigel!'

'I prefer to call it—irony.' He laughed softly. 'Well, well, I've learned a thing or two about women. You can never rely on them. And to think I thought you'd come here to cry over me in this exotic setting and in the isolation that money can buy!'

'Hugo, please, don't listen to him,' Tirza begged again, and then her thoughts turned to ice when he said,

'Look, I'm not given to screaming hysterics, or the screaming that goes along with your peacock dreams, but I am interested in one thing,' he glanced at his watch, 'in five minutes you'll be out of here.' He pushed past them on his way into the hall.

'I've come all this way,' said Nigel. 'Just don't be pokey, Tirza. I've come all this way just to be with you. Isn't that enough?'

Her slap across his cheek took him by surprise and he stumbled backwards, and she took this opportunity to close the heavy door in his face. Sagging against the door, she stood there, with silent tears running down her cheeks, until she heard Nigel's car start and drive off.

When she had control of herself she went in search of Hugo and found him in the indoor patio. He was standing in front of the arched windows, with their ginger and white striped awnings.

'He's gone,' she said, in a diminished voice. 'Please let me explain . . .'

'You intended to go on seeing this man behind my back, all the time, didn't you?' His eyes were like ice.

'No. No, I didn't.'

'And you'd even been to bed with him. The fact that he was a married man meant nothing to you.'

'I have never been to bed with him! I told Nigel about the dream, I tell you. I only *told* him . . . once when we were talking about these things.'

'Save it,' he shrugged. 'I have no intention of believing that, either. You're more calculating than I thought. Anyway, I'm not quite the fool you took me for. You'll come back to Cape Town with me, *before we're married*. To hell with a special licence! Why should I settle for anything second rate—even if you happen to be that—we'll be married in great pomp and style in Cape Town. Papa Harper will lay it on . . . *thick*.'

When he kissed her roughly, relief that he was not leaving her surged through her, cancelling out all reason but this moment and that Hugo was still here with her. 'Hugo,' she said brokenly, 'I—love you.'

He released her suddenly. 'Don't make a stage of this situation, Tirza. It isn't necessary. Can't you understand—I merely want to make love to you.

It's a marriage in the interest of business, after all.'
His voice was brutal, and she shook her head
slowly, as if to throw off all the confusion she was
feeling at this moment.

She spent the rest of the evening alone in her
room, clearing everything from her ivory louvre-
doored cupboards as she intended taking her pos-
sessions back with her to Cape Town. Fortunately,
she thought, with considerable bitterness, there
were cases in which to pack them, left behind by
her father at some time or another.

When she was a small girl, she remembered, and
in fact right up to the present time her father's
expensive luggage always served as a grim reminder
and threat that he would be going off on another
business trip, at a moment's notice, leaving her
behind with only Mrs Meeker and the servants for
company.

She also spent time thinking about what a useless
life she had led, and she brooded on Hugo and
resolutely refused to listen to the small voice that
demanded to know what real future there could be
in this marriage for either of them.

CHAPTER EIGHT

BEFORE they left in the morning, Tirza gazed round the elegant drawing-room. In this room, with the rich golden and bejewelled colours, blue-and-white Delftware in white alcoves on either side of the white fireplace, pieces of brass and copper and Persian carpets on gold carpeting, Hugo had mixed their drinks before dinner at night. It was, she thought wistfully, a room full of memories—some of them good, some of them bad.

'Are you ready?' His voice startled her and she swung round to look at him.

'You—startled me,' she said.

'I'm sorry.' His voice was abrupt.

She began groping in her bag for her sunglasses, but before she put them on, they stood looking at one another . . . strangers, although they had known what it was to be totally absorbed in one another.

'I managed to get my father on the phone, by the way,' she told him. 'He—he knows I'm coming home to be married.'

'I hope you didn't tell him *why* you're to be married,' his voice was hard and mocking. 'It would hardly be fair to tell him that this is your way of starting a very successful weaving industry, along with my know-how and that anything Papa does, Tirza can do better.'

She was wearing black trousers, tight-cut over

her slender hips, and a white shirt with a wide, extravagant collar. Her tawny hair appeared bleached in places by the sun, and her smooth skin was tanned an attractive biscuit brown, but her face was pale. It revealed nothing except a sense of fashion, but her green eyes showed the hurt.

'I was very tactful, don't worry. He took it very well.'

The sun blazed down on the Karroo and its strange compelling solitude. They were leaving the purple and khaki landscape behind and Tirza found herself wondering whether they would ever return, in fact, to the place where, like a cactus flower, she had been content to bask in the warmth of it, with Hugo always close at hand. The weaving industry, which had been so important to her, seemed like a vague dream.

Cape Town bustled with its own affairs, and she realised that she didn't even know where her future husband's office was—let alone his house.

Pigeons flew over the city and strutted about arrogantly on the ledges of buildings. Mist drifted away from the 'tablecloth' and fell in folds down the cliffs of Table Mountain and then, when it reached a certain distance level, it was dissipated by the hotter air below. On top of the mountain, however, the 'cloth' did not grow smaller but remained spread out along its huge bulk.

Douglas Harper was in his study when they arrived and, pausing in the doorway, Tirza said, 'Hi, D.H.' She undid the scarf she had tied about her hair. There was a confused moment and then she said, 'This is Hugo—Hugo Harrington—the man I'm going to marry, D.H.'

'I won't say I'm not surprised.' Douglas Harper looked very handsome with hair the colour of pewter, a tanned face and blazing blue eyes. 'I am.' He held out his hand and the blue eyes went over his future son-in-law. 'So you're going to take my daughter from me, are you?' He looked suddenly stricken, but recovered himself immediately. 'I know I'm seldom home, but it's too late to rectify that. When I *am* at home, though, Tirza is always the first person I look for, believe me. After all, she's the only person in my life.'

Because it was expected of him Hugo said, 'Well, you'll be gaining a son-in-law, after all.'

'I'm surprised to find you at home,' Tirza said, without thinking. 'I mean, I wasn't able to give a specific time, I didn't know quite when we'd arrive.'

'I have a meeting later,' her father answered. 'I won't be free to dine with you, unfortunately.' He glanced at Hugo.

'I hadn't planned on dining here,' Hugo told him. 'You see, my housekeeper has been alerted. She'll be expecting me. I just wanted to deliver your daughter in one piece, safe and sound. She very nearly got trampled by a herd of elephants, however. Didn't you?' He lifted a strand of her hair.

'In Swaziland? You did go to Swaziland first, though, didn't you, before going on to the farm? Where did this happen?'

'Yes, D.H., I did. I met your Cathy, of course, and then we all went on to the Kruger National Park. And Hugo is exaggerating.'

'How did you find her—Cathy, I mean!'

'Oh, fine. Paige, too, of course.' If only you knew, she thought with sudden fury.

The strangest part about everything, Tirza found herself thinking after it was all over, was that Hugo and her father had got along, from the beginning.

Before he had left Hugo had said, 'Lunch tomorrow? You must choose an engagement ring— and a wedding ring to go with it, of course.'

'I hadn't thought about it,' she felt herself begin to fluster.

'Well, I had, as a matter of fact. So be ready, will you?' He kissed her lightly on the mouth.

And then, with her hair drawn back and gathered at the neck in a loose knot and huge sunglasses hiding her eyes and most of her face, she had lunched with him. She was a polished, beautiful woman now, cool and composed, with a shell about her. Outwardly, anyway.

After lunch, she chose an emerald and diamond ring and a plain gold band.

The following evening Hugo surprised her again by turning up without letting her know.

'Gerry Strauss rang me today, at my office. He hadn't been able to contact you or your father,' he told her.

'We were out,' she said, her green eyes widening with fear. 'What did he have to say, Hugo?'

'Don't worry, I have good news for you, Tirza. You can forget about rabid dogs—and all that goes along with them.'

The relief was so great that she was silent for so

long that he said anxiously, taking her by the shoulders, 'Are you all right?'

'Yes,' she whispered, then she began to cry and put her head on his shoulder, but he made no attempt to hold her or to kiss her, and after a while she drew back from him.

'I'm sorry,' she said.

'I think you've been very patient,' he told her, enfolding her with his arms now.

'Well,' she touched her cheeks with her finger-tips, 'coming from *you* that's quite something.'

'I'm not as bad as all that,' Hugo said softly. 'Am I?' He placed his fingers beneath her chin and tilted her face up to his own.

'B-by the way,' she moved away, 'the wedding invitations are being printed and my father has been in touch with the best caterers. Actually, he went to some fuss. Caterers were considered and then discarded, just like that, until he felt quite satisfied.' She had spoken nervously and sounded highly-strung. And then she hurried on, 'It all seems so unreal. I—I'm a fool, Hugo, to be going through with this marriage. It will never work. It is, after all, nothing more than an—arrangement.'

'It's going to be an arrangement that's going to work, and what's more, it will be a permanent arrangement. It's going to be very real and very final, so bank on that for the future,' he told her.

'I think it's a fairly safe assumption to say that I *have* banked on it, and that's what has worried me. I'm not sure about you. I certainly don't want to be married more than once, Hugo.'

'Good. Neither do I,' he said. 'And so we'll have

to make this one work. I want to take you to the house tomorrow. Maggie and Joseph September are looking forward to meeting you.'

'Well, yes, I want to meet them too, of course.'

Her first glimpse of Hugo's house created instant excitement. At an angle she had never seen it before, Table Mountain looked spectacular in the dusk, as it loomed up to one side of the property which was at the end of a long, steep drive.

On the patio there were white tables and chairs, cushioned in rust-coloured material which would, Tirza knew, blend with the pine-wooded slopes of the mountain in the sunshine. Several white plant-holders had tall plants growing in them, with leaves like green bayonets.

The couple who ran Hugo's home for him came out to meet them.

'This is the future Mrs Harrington,' Hugo told them, smiling. 'Tirza, I've told you about Maggie and Joseph September.'

For a few moments they stood talking about the view and the garden, of which Joseph September was very proud, and the tension eased a little. Hugo then guided Tirza up three wide steps to the verandah where black, intricately-scrolled wrought-iron chairs were cushioned in black, patterned with outsize red flowers and vivid green leaves. Sliding doors were open to the lounge, which exuded warmth and sophistication.

Tirza's gaze roved about the room. 'It's beautiful,' she said. There was a magnificent copper canopy over the fireplace and the carved base of the low table was, quite obviously, a Mexican antique. The sofas on either side of the fireplace were low-slung and covered in oatmeal coloured tweed and this material was repeated in the curtaining, forming an excellent background for the blending of peach, melon and pistachio on off-white carpeting. Identical lamps stood on low tables at either end of the stone fireplace, which stretched the width of one wall.

'So this is to be my new home,' she murmured.

'Do you like it—so far?' Hugo's voice was abrupt.

'Yes, very much.'

'In that case, we'll have a drink. I've told Maggie we won't be eating here, we'll eat in town. Okay?'

'Yes, of course.' Her teeth were chattering and she bit her lip.

'I'll show you around later.'

From one of the sofas she watched him as he went to a cupboard to pour their drinks and then Maggie came into the room, carrying a tray of savouries, and when she had gone Hugo said, 'By the way, what would you like to drink?' It was all very formal, she thought.

'I'd love a Cinzano, if you have it,' she told him.

'I do have it.'

As he passed her the glass their fingertips touched.

'You've changed your perfume today,' Hugo observed.

'Yes, I have.' Was that all he had to say? she found herself thinking.

And then, as she sat sipping at her drink and settled in an elegant heap of soft apricot silk pleats

in the corner of the oatmeal wool sofa, her eyes
met his, over the rim of the glass.

'Well, seeing that I have no desire of engaging in
an affair with you until after we're married, Miss
Harper, what shall we talk about?' His blue eyes
were mocking as they went over her. 'Although I
could make love to you here and now, make no
mistake about that.'

'I don't know,' she replied, in a stiff little voice.
'Somehow we've become strangers—so what about
people being hijacked in planes, or handsome, kidnapped diplomats? That would always do to start.'

'You know what they say,' he went on looking
at her.

'No. What do they say?'

'They say that strangers become friends and in
turn, friends become lovers.'

'Really? Well, I always try not to expect too
much.'

'Does that mean that you want me to love you?
Tonight?' He went on studying her.

'I'm not sure what I want,' Tirza replied in a
small voice. 'Certainly not tonight.' She began to
shake.

'Why are you shaking?' Hugo asked.

'I'm not.' She swallowed her drink in one gulp.
'I'd love another drink. May I?' she tried to make
her voice sound light. 'I *do* know what I want,
though. All I ask for is a settled and controlled
way of life.'

He came for her glass. 'And you think you're
going to get that with me?' There was interest in
his voice.

'I'm not sure.' Her face was slightly hostile.

A city view glittered in the distance and when she remarked on it he offered to show her the rest of the house. 'I love the house,' she told him, afterwards.

'If you have anything besides clothes you'd like to have sent over, go ahead,' he told her. 'In fact, just let me know and I'll make arrangements about transport.'

Tirza laughed suddenly. 'You wouldn't say that if you knew just what I do have! I've never lived in a house this old,' she went on, 'and yet it looks so—*new*. Just imagine, it's a house steeped in history we don't know about. It's not haunted, is it?' She turned to look at him and, for a seemingly endless moment, their eyes remained locked and she thought Hugo was going to kiss her.

'No, you can set your mind at rest on that score. It used to be a farm and this house was a labourer's cottage.' She watched him as he went to pour himself another drink.

'History always seems older in Cape Town. Do you know, Hugo,' she added, 'I know practically nothing about you.'

'What is it you want to know?' He glanced at her.

'Your parents? Where are they?'

'My father is dead. My mother is in Scotland, right now. I think you'll like her.' Suddenly he smiled. 'What's more, I think your father is going to like her. Somehow,' he shrugged, 'I can imagine them together.'

'Really?' Tirza sounded excited.

'We'll have to wait and see. She's flying back for the wedding.'

'Oh, Hugo! How marvellous!' Suddenly she felt like crying. 'I'm so glad,' she said, very softly.

The forthcoming days, for her, were busy and hectic. While she was at home she found herself missing Hugo acutely. Wedding invitations were sent out and then Hugo's mother arrived. Tirza, realising that she was going to be under inspection, felt herself becoming tense, but she need not have worried, because Sheila Harrington soon put her at ease and she realised, immediately, that the look of both sincerity and gaiety that shone from those smiling blue eyes, so much like Hugo's, would prove a common meeting-point for them both. What was also so marvellous that it had been 'Sheila' and 'Douglas', from the start, and Tirza watched her father with tender amusement.

'I see what you meant about my father and your mother,' she said once.

Everything built up to that moment when she was married to Hugo in a stone church which had been sheltered by oak trees for a hundred years.

There was thinly-veiled curiosity from many of Hugo's friends, not to mention her own. Between them, they had caused quite a stir.

Before leaving for the church her father had caused her to cry a little when he said, 'I never got over loving your mother. In fact, I've always blamed myself for her death, merely for having taken her to India. I'm not trying to make excuses for my behaviour, but I felt driven to do something—and I did. I made money and I went on making money. It should have reached a limit, once I'd reached my goal, but it didn't. I'm not asking you to understand, and I don't expect you to, it's too late for that, but I want you to know that, in my own clumsy way, I've always loved you. I hope you're going to be very happy with Hugo. I like his mother, by the way.'

Smiling, she had said, through her tears, 'You do?'

'Yes. Something makes me think you've brought more than just a son-in-law into my life, Tirza.'

Outwardly, it seemed a perfect wedding and, wearing a free-falling Quiana chiffon creation in a pale coppery apricot shade, which suited her colouring, Tirza went from table to table with Hugo at her side, talking to her friends and meeting his.

They were leaving for the Seychelle Islands the following day. Their cases were packed.

While they were dancing Hugo said, over the noise of conversation and music, 'Well, and what shall we talk about, Mrs Harrington?' They could have been quite alone and he looked into her eyes. There was a kind of animal magnetism about him, Tirza thought, even in his conservative dark suit, which did little to disguise the dangerous, compelling quality about him.

After a moment she said, 'It's unfair to put the onus on me. You tell me what we should talk about.'

He held her closer and said against her ear, 'What about people being hijacked in planes? Or, better still, handsome kidnapped diplomats. Or . . .

what about us? Do you see yourself being married to me?' His voice was touched with humour.

'I *am* married to you now,' she replied, on a shaken note.

'You're very beautiful and you're married to me. You can't expect this to be a casual marriage, Tirza.'

It was after midnight when they drove to his cottage, in a world removed from the confusion of the city. It was a brisk night, clear and glittering with stars. Table Mountain looked vast and haunting, somehow. Lights sprinkled the distant shoreline, like fireflies.

'A setting for a seduction,' said Hugo, helping her from the car.

When they were in the lounge she took off her shoes and flopped down on one of the sofas. 'My eyelids feel as if they're working on two hinges! After almost two hours of participating in my own wedding festivities and making polite conversation and manipulating the kind of smiles to go along with it, I feel utterly drained.' She knew that she was shivering slightly and she knew why.

'Is this your way of trying to delay the inevitable?' He sounded annoyed.

Moodily she watched him. He was superbly tailored but, nevertheless, bore the stamp of arrogance she had grown to know so well. The combination was one of dynamic masculinity. His face was a mask, but his eyes were searching.

'By the way,' the shivering was growing worse, 'I usually have the peacock in the jungle dream when I'm overwrought, or overtired—or run down, even . . .'

He listened impatiently and then cut her short, 'And I take it that this is your way of reminding me that your dream has been shared with Nigel Wright and, no doubt, countless others. You can tell me now. After all, shared intimacies, one way and another, are an integral part of married life.'

Her green eyes reflected the insult. 'I merely want you to know that Nigel Wright was purposely misleading you when he spoke about it. Nigel is a rotter. I merely *told* him about this dream. At one stage, I didn't care what you thought, but now we're married I want to get this straight.'

She watched him as he went in the direction of the drinks cupboard, where he poured a measure of Scotch into a glass, added a splash of soda and ice-cubes from the portable refrigerator which was built into the unit. He glanced up. 'Drink this,' he said. 'Why are you shaking?'

'I'm shaking because I happen to be upset and nervous,' she told him. 'Is it so very unreasonable for me to want to convince you that I'm not what you believe me to be?'

'I'm not what you believe me to be, for that matter,' Hugo snapped. 'For instance, you haven't exactly married a poor man. Your father's money means damn all to me. I married you because I want *you*. Nothing else.'

He brought two glasses over to where she was sitting and placed them on the low coffee table.

'You don't have to say these things,' she said quickly.

'I've said it because I mean it. I say this with

savaged pride,' he said seriously, 'I haven't treated you kindly and I'm sorry. I love you.' He reached for her hands and pulled her up to him.

'When did you decide that?' She made no attempt to hide the bitterness in her voice. '*Now*? Because you—*want* me?'

'I've waited for you,' he told her, 'the girl I wanted for my own, and yet when you came into my life, I didn't recognise you. From the beginning, almost, I realised that you were an heiress, and so far as I was concerned, I was not going to contribute to any of your many "irons in the fire". I couldn't make out what was inside Tirza Theron Harper before I realised I loved her, and then I wanted you on any terms.'

'Oh, Hugo, what kept you silent?' she asked, in a small distressed voice.

'Pride.' His lashes dropped, as his eyes went to her mouth.

'Do you honestly believe I agreed to marry you for business reasons? So that I could gain the know-how to start a weaving industry?' She drew away from him and made an impatient gesture, as if it was all too much for her. 'Do you think any girl would do that?'

'Why did you agree to marry me, then?'

'Oh, can't you *see*? I love you, so I swallowed all my pride, Hugo. You're such a fool . . .'

'Not such a fool.' Tanned and vital, in his dark suit, he reached for her, and she came to him with the abandon of a goddess. Response surged through her, cancelling out everything but their wedding night. With closed eyes she felt him draw away from her and slip out of his jacket which he tossed across the back of the sofa. The way in which he did it was dynamically masculine, and then she was in his arms again and she felt herself being lifted up and carried from the room.

'Don't take my love lightly, Hugo,' she whispered.

'I love you too much for that,' he answered.

Two glasses stood, forgotten, on the low table with the Mexican antique base.

Harlequin® Plus
A WORD ABOUT THE AUTHOR

Wynne May was born in South Africa, ten miles from Johannesburg. Shortly after graduation from college, she began working for the South African Broadcasting Corporation, and it was while on holiday from the S.A.B.C. that she met her husband.

How did it happen? Let Wynne tell it. It's pure Harlequin Romance:

"I had gone to the home of my mother's parents—in Ardeer, on the south coast of Natal. This was *the* place for surfing and swimming. Claude, recently wounded in the Battle of El Alamein, was on leave.

"The scene was set: a blustery day with the sea bounding in and the sand whipping up to sting the face and limbs. Apart from Claude, the beach was utterly deserted. Claude was lounging near the shallow end of a pool.

"Taking the greatest care not to pass in front of the handsome stranger, I took the long way around the pool ... and promptly slipped on the cement and splashed into the water. It is not surprising, therefore, that the young man with the mocking green eyes spoke to me."

Three months later, Claude slipped a diamond ring onto Wynne's finger as they stood under the stars in an exotic garden.

When their son Gregory was eight and Wynne was pregnant with Julian, she decided to write. She completed her first novel just before she went into the hospital.

Before long, Wynne May was looking after two sons, running a home—and writing romances.